LOVELY IN HER BONES

LOVELY IN HER BONES

J. JILL ROBINSON

ARSENAL PULP PRESS
Vancouver, Canada

ARSENAL PULP PRESS
100-1062 Homer Street
Vancouver, B.C.
Canada V6B 2W9

The publisher gratefully acknowledges the assistance of the Canada Council and the Cultural Services Branch, B.C. Ministry of Tourism and Minister Responsible for Culture.

Author photo by Allen Rees
Typeset by the Vancouver Desktop Publishing Centre
Printed and bound in Canada by Hignell Printing

Some of the stories in this collection have been previously published: "Finding Linette" in *Event*, 1992; "Loved Daughter" in *Letters to You* (Second Wednesday Press), 1990; "Lovely in Her Bones" (early version) in *Dandelion*, 1992. A version of "Fairbanks" was broadcast on CBC Radio's "Alberta Anthology" in 1993. The title *Lovely in Her Bones* is from "I Knew a Woman" by Theodore Roethke (1958).

The author wishes to thank Barbara Scott, good editor and friend.

CANADIAN CATALOGUING IN PUBLICATION DATA:
Robinson, Jacqueline Jill, 1955-
  Lovely in her bones

ISBN 0-88978-260-1

  I. Title.
PS8585.035166L6 1993   C813'.54   C93-091027-3
PR9199.3.R62L6 1993

CONTENTS

Lovely in Her Bones is dedicated to my sisters.

—*J.J.R.*

FAIRBANKS

IN SEPTEMBER AND EARLY October, before it gets dark too early, I ride my bike in bright sun. To the university, along bike paths, across a big field with a railway crossing, beside the experimental farm in whose fields I see the 'Frankencows.' The wooden stoppers in their sides jiggle up and down as the untroubled cows walk, or stand chewing.

I am always alone. Always thinking. In, and in, and in unto myself. I tell you, the world is the inside of my head. And I think one day, only I, in the whole wide world, am thinking these thoughts, feeling these feelings, right now. Here are the turning leaves and the blue sky, and the crisp air, and birds, and trees, and none of it knows or cares anything at all about me, and if I were obliterated they would remain exactly the same. Get things into perspective, woman.

In the big field one morning in late September two sand cranes take flight, sever from earth beside me. Drop not a crumb of land as they change elements. This occurrence feels important, like an omen—my aloneness under vast, vast sky, the two of them so near me shifting easily, readily, from earth to air.

That same day, in the afternoon, after school, I go for a run along Chena Pump Road. Work at losing myself in the rhythms of my body moving, in my breathing, work on this physical awareness of self aside from mere shadow outline. So I make it inside, inside my breathing and my thoughts. I glance up. There in front of me, in the golden autumn, out Chena Pump Road in Fairbanks, Alaska, on a black, asphalt bike path, is a monk. A monk, in purple robes. They look lovely against the turning birch leaves. A Tibetan monk, with a round brown head and face. Beatific expression and all. Good Morning, he says.

A matter of seconds. In which I slow in a sudden, amazed mixture of courtesy and astonishment. I manage to smile.

You can see how I could think the day auspicious. Can't blame me, fault me for that now, can you? At first I try to will the cranes and the monk into adding up to your presence, a sudden and magical appearance like theirs. But you don't know I am in Alaska. I haven't talked to you in a year; how could you know? And so I settle on a letter. I will write to you.

I tell you: Sunsets are great here before winter. Four, three, two in the afternoon. Across the sweep of the Tanana Valley the pinks and oranges spread.

I tell you: Alaska is a big place. It is the way the whole world used to be. Unsullied, mostly. It's all that's left. For now. That is left—that remains. That is left—left alone. For now.

Flying autumn colours. And so am I. Dark green and golden.

I don't write.

Fade into winter.

Black. White. The only colour is in memory—the monk's purple robe.

Stir to grey and chill. Freeze hard, all the way through. Lakes rivers trees cars outhouses.

Layer me in longjohns. Undershirts, sweaters and down. Bulk me up with scarves. Mittens. Balaclava. Under all this soft padding something hard and aching and hungry. With sharp edges, and dense as iron ore.

Socked into winter. Hell frozen over. I buy a trapper's hat, beaver, with a wolverine's tail. I layer against ice fog and snow. I meet Susan Butcher at a dog sled meet. I go on a dog sled ride. I see the moons of Jupiter through a gigantic telescope. I watch the aurora skitter across the sky. I want to be against your skin just once more, even with this winter skin dry as a desert snake's.

I have a great uncle who suffered from unrequited love. Uncle Gilbert. He went crazy. Not from the love, however; the going nuts was result rather than cause of the purple heart of the trouble. I think. He bought a girl a ring, had decided to marry her, and she turned him down. Viola was her name. He made the whole thing up, you see. And in the attempt to translate his wish into the tangible—not the real, for it was real—perception, you know—the wish didn't make it. Shattered. He was sent to an asylum, in Guelph, and when he came back he wasn't the same. From then on he liked to tell children stories that made them weep.

He became a hermit. He moved to his father's hunting lodge near Fort Garry. There were no dogs (they raised English setters) or horses by then; just the lodge, the brook, the trees. His sister visited sometimes. Brought him food. She worried.

When I was small and romantic, I loved having had a hermit in the family.

That was before I knew what it meant to be touched. And not touched.

I have had so little touching in my life.

My cabin is down a crisscross of lanes named King Arthur, Guinevere, Lancelot. Out my cabin door I see birch. Endless straight poles black and white.

As winter goes on, or, rather, endures—for it doesn't proceed, or progress, it just moves in, in a solid block, and sits like a boulder—I spend time thinking about us. (I was going to say in the middle of the night. But the middle is so deep, when the night starts at two and goes on until noon.) In that thick blackness, starry only if I go outside, I think about my experience. With you.

I remember saying to the gods, Just once. Please let it happen, just once, let me borrow, just borrow him, one single time. I won't be greedy. I'll be good ever after.

The bargain was struck.

If I go outside, stand under crisp clean stars, shiver staring, waiting, hoping for the aurora, and if I see it, that sense of insignificance I felt while riding my bike to school might well sweep over me again. None of this knows or cares what's gnawing at me. None of this is affected by my night of lust with you. That is alien to this cold, these stars, if not completely to the shiver of movement through the starry pelt of the aurora.

You stood at my door and I pushed it open wider to let you in. God, when you touched me. Not a word.

Warm warm hands underneath my chemise.

I have never felt that way before or since. Let me tell you that.

And then you went home.

Dead of winter. In the loft I pile pillows high and rest my chin on them. I look down at the door, at the furnace, at the windows you can't see through, heavy with ice and snow. I think about that monk. Right now he is meditating, perhaps. Lighting incense. Not lonely. Outside, my tank full of fuel. Winter. Thirty-seven below out there. Fahrenheit, of course. And will be fifty-seven soon. My little car is plugged in, but it will run like a brittle tin can in this weather, a tin can with macaroni doors and squared off tires.

Did you know there is a temperature at which antifreeze will freeze?

For a solid year the memory of that once has stayed so strong. Vividly I have seen and felt your face, your hands, your cock. Roused, aroused, with just the curl tipped beginning of the *idea* of the memory. Just thinking about the door, for goodness sake, has got me going.

And then what.

Hope? Hope is a small town on the Kenai peninsula. It is a pretty place, with many old houses. Quaint. The village was closed when I was there, late at night, early next morning. I don't know what caused the village.

Near the campground is a high, foreboding cliff. You might climb down but you would never get back up. It is far, far down. The ocean at the bottom is not friendly or tame. You cannot see through the water; it is muddy, turmoiled, roiled water and gritty, grey sand. You would not like to fall down there, I tell you. Hope is a purple cliff.

Fling—what an old-fashioned word.

Melt into spring.
My remembering evolves over the winter. I have begun to think that perhaps it was the event more than the you that I continue to miss. That still presses against a sore place inside me. When I think about it.
I miss the experience, then, not the person. Is that cruel? It makes you a vehicle, you see. The way. Metalust. Translove airlines. Through, by way of, via. Metaphysical lust, baby.

You have gradually faded away. Some parts have stayed longer than others.

The days grow long and sunny. They stretch almost too long now. Light. My skin soaks up light. I feel like a flower, a sponge, a satellite dish sucking up sun signals. Isn't there some fabric that soaks up light? Then emits some slightly in a glow?
The days seemed, in some ways, longer when I was in the dark. But they are both twenty-four hours. It is the light that makes the difference, the light that interprets length. Rhythms of human activity that attempt to be reflected in the wane and woof of light and dark. Or perception. I couldn't see in the winter. I can see, now that it is summer for sure. More than I want to, sometimes. Need wooden slats for my windows to keep it all out. Movie star facial

masks to cover my eyes when I sleep. Lacy and tied with a ribbon.

I am a hermit now, I suppose. In my cabin, in my woods. I have a patchwork quilt. I don't have a cat, but I might some day. I have an outhouse with powder blue netting for a curtain. (It looks as though a ballet dancer were caught in the door and tore herself away.) I have two big water jugs full by the door. I have a computer on my kitchen table.

I sit on my porch and smack large mosquitoes.

Naked under a cheesecloth gown, I stand in the doorway.

I'm fully aware of how sucky it sounds to have the sun come out so steadily, long, and completely to parallel my own feeling better. I cannot, however, manipulate nature to make the parallel more original. This is the way it is. Here in Fairbanks, anyway.

ALVA
AND
ME

EARLIER TODAY, BONNY dropped off some stuff, but she didn't ring the doorbell. I found the bag—or paper sack, as the Americans say—when I went out to check for the paper. (The paper boy is a moron, Alva says. Says she wrote a letter to the paper—the *Mustang Daily News Miner*—News Minus, she calls it, or Mindless—commending them for hiring the mentally handicapped, but suggesting they give him a less responsible job.) The boy was still halfway down the block. At what Alva and Bonny call the slums, I could see his flashlight bobbing. Cheap empty townhouses that no one will rent except the kind of university students who trash places and make so much noise the state troopers have to be called in.

But there on the step was this bag filled with Crisco,

margarine, whipping cream, mashed potato mix, and pie crust mix. And in the newspaper box was a bag of white miniature marshmallows. Frozen solid, of course. The whipping cream, too. This is twenty-seven below and falling we're talking here, which, in Fairbanks, is still pretty moderate. The little marshmallows reminded me of the ear plugs I've started to use so I don't wake up and hear Alva coughing and choking. Hear her coughing so hard it turns into retching. It makes me almost puke.

Bonny is Alva's drinking buddy down the street, and since Alva was sick on Thanksgiving, they're having the dinner today. Alva will make up the sweet potatoes, the pumpkin pie, the mince. She, Alva the Great, has been doing it for years, she tells Bonny. Nothing that she couldn't do blindfolded. The reason Bonny has never tasted any really good pie, by the way—even if she thinks she has—is because she isn't from the South. It takes a Southerner to make good crust. I thought it just took Crisco, says Bonny. My ass, says Alva.

Bonny calls a couple of hours later to see if Alva got the stuff okay. Just to help you out on a couple of steps, if you want, she says. Alva is disgusted. Mixes, she says to me. Mixes, for Thanksgiving dinner. No chance.

Alva offered me her spare room this semester. For nominal rent. She is, she says, afraid of "the big one"—a heart attack that'll polish her off. Having company will help, she says. My job is to call 911. If necessary. I'm not sure how I'll hear through the ear plugs, but in the meantime, I've got to sleep.

I'll be gone December 15th, and then what she'll do I don't know.

Last week Alva moved her bed. Took her all afternoon, and she didn't ask for a hand. Moved it, slid it, budged it over so that now she can lie in bed and watch her TV. She likes that TV. Before I got my ear plugs I'd hear it in the middle of the night, hear it blare out prices on the shopping channel. Or I'd hear cartoons. Ghostbusters. Flintstones. Or movies. Nature shows. Stalking the swan-bellied pink egret in eastern Ohio.

There is a Bob Dylan brass bed in my room. It was her great grandparents', she says, and then her husband's. I hope he didn't die in it. He did die in one of these beds, three years ago, of a heart attack. An anthropology student studying death shouldn't be so queasy.

Also in my room is Alva's mother's hope chest, which Alva had refinished last year, and which I have been cautioned not to scratch. Not to put anything on. Alva's grandfather's rock collection is in my room too. Behind glass. And a big black trunk that sits under the window. Black leather. Brass corners and locks. A body would fit in that trunk.

On the trunk is a vase, actually a pitcher, filled with dried flowers. It comes from Tennessee. A copper-coloured hound curves for the handle. Draped down the sides of the pitcher itself are dead pheasants and rabbits, a fox, a duck. All hanging by their feet, which curl and end at the pitcher's mouth. Copper-coloured too, these corpses lie against a colour of green you'd get mixing pond algae with coal dust.

None of it exactly constitutes a pleasant scene. Thank you I'd *love* another lemonade. *Such* a quaint vase.

There isn't a mark of me in the place. I'm in two drawers and the gigantic walk-in closet. My three pairs of jeans. My sweatshirts. My turtlenecks. My socks, undershirts, panties, and thermal underwear, mitts, and scarves. That's it. Except for a few books, and a laptop computer. Alva likes that I have so little, I think. Her charity is all the more worthwhile if I am without.

I am invited for Thanksgiving dinner with her and Bonny and, I suppose, Bonny's family, but decline, though I wouldn't mind catching a glimpse of Bonny and her husband in action. Alva has told me they are a real pair. They call each other by terms of endearment like "asshole," and "shithead." With true affection, Alva says. It's just their way. Nice way, I say.

Alva is sure the dinner won't be my kind of thing anyway, and she's right. She thinks I won't like all the rowdiness, all the drunkenness and tomfoolery. This is because she thinks I am straight and virtuous. This façade has always served me well. Actually, I don't want to go because I don't like being all smiley and noddy to people I don't know and don't want to know and will never meet again, all for the sake of stuffing myself on a turkey dinner. I already had a dinner anyway, at a grad student party on the official Thanksgiving Day. Alva stayed home and drank.

That's what she spends her time doing, and it takes up a lot of time if you commit yourself to doing it right. Time consuming. Time plus consuming. Meet your quota. I know whereof I speak. I've been there. Well, not there, perhaps, not there where Alva is, but I've been part of the way.

With Alva, it's usually vodka. The old lie that you can't smell it on your breath so it isn't there even if you see it in the eyes, the skin, the stance. She switches to gin, which she bought for when Bonny comes over, only when she runs out of vodka. Quick trips to the corner store are not always possible. Especially if you're three-quarters thwacked and need just enough to finish yourself off for the night, or day, or whatever the hell time it is.

Bonny got nailed with a DWI this past summer and had to spend three whole days in jail, so the both of them are scared to drive, though they get braver after every drink. I *have* heard the Mercedes fire up and the garage door open at all kinds of hours, and I know what's up. And if it's in the day time and I'm around, I know not to sit in the kitchen, because that's where she'll unload the bottles, and I shouldn't be there to see. I'm aware of her feelings.

The telephone can be a bone of contention between us. Alva doesn't like it to ring for anyone but her. It doesn't ring much for anyone, in actual fact. But if it's for me, she calls me by a wrong name out the door, Lydia! Linda! or says I'm not home and I have to scramble to convince her it's not so. When I moved in, she said, It would be better if you were home to receive your phone calls. I'll try, I said.

On Thursday nights, if he doesn't forget or isn't busy doing something else, the phone rings and it is my husband.

He asks me how my studies are going. I ask him how the dog is, how the house is, if he remembered to pay the bills. He tells me there isn't too much happening. I get the impression that the world will kick in when I get home. Meanwhile, it is in a state of suspension. Usually I cry after these phone calls. They have such little substance. I sit and cry and wonder if our whole marriage has such little substance.

Any time now the door to Alva's bedroom will open and out she'll come to head downstairs to start her cooking. Her recipe books are spread out all over the kitchen counters for me to see. The pumpkin pie recipe. The pastry recipe. The yam recipe.

Yesterday I went to see the dogsled races with a writer friend I met at the Howling Dog bar. Sam. We danced. I haven't danced in a decade. My husband is a books-and-chairs, exchange-smiles-now-and-again sort.

People wake up different parts of you. Some people wake up this; other people wake up that. Makes you start to wonder just how much more there is to you that never *ever* gets woken up when you get surprises like that dancing at the Dog.

The big sled dogs are for long distance, a girl told me—more so for the Quest than for the Iditarod, because the Quest is so hilly, and it is so long between check stations. The small dogs are for sprinting. (Is that right? Or have I got them backwards?) The first team we saw had the dogs' names in indelible ink on their harnesses. Snowflake. Frosty. Rusty. One the colour of a fox, that soft red, like the ruff of a parka. What breeding lines do that? I asked. Touch of red setter, the girl said. Friendly dogs, waggy dogs. Tough, durable dogs. Some, after the race, with blood-coloured saliva frozen into their whiskers and icicles down their jowls. Their tongues hang out to sweat, she said. And touch the cold metal snap on the line, and bits of their tongue come off, and so they bleed.

Sam's from Boston, Little Rock, and Los Angeles. He is teaching here at the University for a year. We banter well. God, a man who *talks*. We talk about the end of the world; we talk about the Berlin Wall; we talk about writing; we talk about damn near everything. In fact, I dreamed about him last night. I dreamed we were in Vancouver or somewhere, where he was living, and he was giving me a ride home in his Toyota. I suggested we go for a cappuccino. And it was dark in the car at one point, and for some reason, fate, I suppose, our faces turned and our mouths met not because either of us intended to kiss the other, but because our faces were so close together that it just happened. And the kiss was soft and short. And another. And another. And then that bit of challenge came into it; that rebutting inviting kind of kissing that turns you on. Or turns me on, anyway. Oh shit. It was a great dream, but awfully far from the truth.

If I start dating again, Alva says sometimes. If I remarry. And sometimes I think it is sad, and how lonely she must be, and how nice for her that would be, and other times I think who the hell is going to put up with you and your habits? I mean, the cleaning lady comes and after she goes Alva runs around, or moves around, anyway, making sure that the little gold-dipped glass ornaments that have been moved a sixteenth of an inch are back where they belong. That the rug is absolutely centre. That the pictures are all straight. Not that the cleaning woman missed doing one of the bathrooms, or that the cupboards need a good wipe down or she ignored the stove. Just that the toaster is lined up right against the wall, and the Kleenex boxes face the right way in all the rooms.

She's told me that I'm a good student to have since I'm married. She couldn't handle three things, she says. Marijuana, a messy person, or a person who had strange men popping out of the bedroom and seeing her in her nightgown. This is her house, after all. Yes, I said. I can understand that.

Alva's living room isn't somewhere my writer friend and I could visit comfortably anyway. Alva's sister lived in Germany a long time ago and bought this two-hundred-year-old furniture and shipped it home. Then she got strapped for money, and Alva bought the stuff from her. Ornately carved black wood with gold paint highlights. Pink and light blue embroidered satin upholstery you'd die if you spilled anything on. Just recovered last year, Alva says. Look out. There are two wing chairs, a settee, and a dining room suite, and none of it you want to sit on. There's just one place to sit. Other than the floor, that is. A big red fake leather recliner that was her husband's. This I sit in sometimes, when I get sick of sitting in my room staring out into the darkness watching the snow fall. A change of scenery. It's rather like sitting on a stage set. Everything dazzles you at first, and then you start really looking around. Yes, those are really two Hogarths up there on the wall, but they're placed right above a grouping of plastic seals and a plastic ivory walrus on the big old stereo console.

My writer friend Sam would like to see this place for material, he says.

The house is always silent, though Alva has told me that she loves music. There is a formidable record collection, but it never moves; those records never go around. Nothing in the house even squeaks or makes noise, except for me (my husband would say here, I suppose, that it's a well-laid floor that hasn't a single squeak). Listen hard and you can hear the movement of her feet against the carpet, her hand along the handrail, the cupboard doors open and close, the refrigerator open and close.

I've started watching the vodka bottles. I can tell if it's been a long night or a short night. The vodka bottles are mood indicators.

There is a picture of Alva with her husband by the front door. Alva has long black hair. Alva looks as though she looked pretty darn good in her forties. Her husband is older, by a good fifteen years. It is their wedding day.

Looking at Alva today, it seems a lot longer ago than it really is. Her face is mottled, swollen, red from drink. Her black hair shines falsely, dyed though she says it isn't, straggly and thinning like witch hair. Her stomach is monstrously bloated. She looks a ruined mid-sixties. She is fifty-three, I think.

Alva is how I'd be if I kept up living the way I was living before I married my husband, and if I continued to increase my habits for a good few years after. Smoking a pack a day and drinking three bottles of wine or a good dose of vodka. He knew me when everything revolved around the liquor store and money to get enough. And at thirty I started cleaning up my act and it's five years now and I'm grateful that he loved me through all that and never said one word against me or what I was doing. He loved me anyway. He loved me in spite of all that.

So what if he doesn't talk much? So what if he doesn't send shivers up the back? What the hell do you want in this life, girl? Everything? You're never going to have everything. Be glad someone loves you. Be glad someone loves you, whatever that means.

The only touch of flesh I have had in three months is touching Sam's hand as I pass him the joint in the car. Then we put our gloves back on. We are up Rosie Creek Road, looking out over the frozen, white Tanana River. There are cross country skiers. There is a dog. There is a snow machine. We watch, side by side. Even when I cry he pats the down shoulder of my parka with a gloved hand. With my mitt I pat his red shoulder and tell him he is a good guy. A good guy. Where are those mouths that just happen to be so close together? We stare at the Tanana and smile at each other and then he takes me home to Alva's house. I had fun, I say, as I always say. I had fun. You drive carefully now.

Some days my husband's face is closer than others. Some days I can almost forget about him. Other days, days when I might be imagining being touched by my writer friend, there he is, not damning, not condemning, not even looking hurt. I am here and I am waiting for you and the world has stopped until you come back. Period.

Alva has decided to use the stuff that Bonny brought over, since she doesn't want to make the trip to Safeway. And then from the back of a cupboard lo and behold canned yams. Jars of mincemeat. Cans of pumpkin. The biscuits she will still make from scratch. She'll make them at Bonny's, though, because they will get cold in the minus thirty-whatever and the twenty-five yards between the two townhouses. And Lord only knows when she'll get home. Sometimes it isn't until the next day.

Sam is stopping by tonight. I've promised him a tour of this place. And then I don't know what we'll do. Tonight. This week. Next week.

MEMORIES
ARE MADE
OF THIS

As THE FERRY MANEUVRES among the islands, Garret and Lea see two bald eagles at the tops of two tall trees almost three hundred yards apart. Through the binoculars they watch one feeding the young, the other sentry up high, watching. Each on a fir tall and twisted, bonzaied by the wind.

I didn't know they were so big. Just look at them.

I didn't know they were so big. Let me have another look, would you? Over and over, in awe until they pass.

Did you get a picture? Garret asks.

Can't he see she doesn't have her camera out? Why is it always she who is supposed to have everything ready and at hand?

No. Did you?

Nope.

She's not sure why she invited him; things are hardly improving between them. He's as silent as ever; as passive as ever. What do you want to do, Garret? Whatever, Lea. He's always so unwilling to risk the first move. It makes him as hard as a barnacle sometimes.

She insisted on this island; any one would be fine as far as he was concerned. She has been here before. Several times. When she was very small, she came with her parents, she told him. Later, with a boyfriend, Phil. There is plenty of nostalgia associated with this place for her.

Garret, however, isn't especially one for what he calls sentiment, she has noticed. He doesn't like to talk about his family, or his childhood. He apparently has no store of memories the way she does, no warehouse for the past; in fact his memory is rather poor. What he does remember about his childhood seems to be in sepia shadows, and it must taste like mud. As though, like the flats by the Deas Island tunnel, it were all fenced and labelled DANGER: QUICKSAND.

Last time she asked about his family, he said, summarily, uncharacteristically coldly, The ones that matter are dead. And the others ought to be. I don't want anything to do with them.

Do you have a choice? she asked then, intentionally prodding. Is it something you can decide? Maybe you just think you can forget all about them. That's what I think—I could never get away from my family, dead or living, even if I wanted to. They're always around. Defining me.

Well I've done a pretty good job of convincing myself. Let's leave it at that.

They set up camp by the twisted arbutus and the sea. Above them, a haze of grey clouds looks as though it won't hang around. The cliff falls away to the sea, down to a rocky beach. The water gently ripples, ruffled, up the inlet.

Soon Garret goes down to the beach. Standing on the cliff, she can see him move farther and farther away, until she can no longer see the turquoise on his thongs, his red windbreaker. He likes to pick things up, touch them. Textures. In his job he encourages builders to put textures in their houses, in stucco, in stickle, in wallpaper and wood. Here he picks up anything, everything, that catches this eye for touch, that might be good to feel. Constantly up and down he bends from the waist, bends from the knees, too, in a spidery plié. Only occasionally he slips something into a pocket.

Eventually she too goes down to the beach, walks the other way onto stretches of stone. Drying seaweed, limpets' shells dry and warm, their creatures underneath sucked hard onto stone. She crouches down and dips her hands into hot salt water pools, peers into dark crannies. Bright orange and flaming red slimy things the shape of limp cocks lie in narrow slits of grey rock. Piles of plump, hard, orange and purple starfish stacked stuck on top of each other, dozens of them, waiting for the tide in cool crevices, jammed between slabs of stone. Anemones, mostly white. Small green pickles with hot pink daisy centres. In the pools, dying barnacles gasp in their cruel little houses. Oh let the tide come; let the tide come soon and save me. Assure one more tidal turn of life. Their slithery silver tongues flicker in and out of sharp shells into the hot water. Dying crabs float pale belly up.

Something uneasing about these creatures of a different element. Slid into slits, skittering or sucking.

She spent afternoons crouched like this when she was a child. Lifted up stones and watched the crabs run. Poked into the soft mouths of anemones to make them close against her finger or stick.

It's been a long time now. She never gets to the beach. Her practice is busy—and so requires an utter commitment she isn't always sure she wants to give. Recently it has required particularly long hours, and she continued to work hard because what would happen if she didn't was much less clear than what would happen if she did. Finally there is some calm.

Garret is in this calm.

Waiting.

I'm sure glad things have slowed down, Lea.

Why? What did you have in mind?

Oh, I hadn't given it much thought. Any ideas?

Sure, but you first.

She is getting sick of this game. And she is starting to get mean.

Her great uncle, her grandfather's brother, lived in Peace River before moving to the coast and then to this island, she tells Garret. She knows little about the Peace country or his time up there, because she hadn't really cared at a time when anyone remembered. This is what growing old does for you, she says. Isn't it? Makes you obsessive about remembering and trying to remember; fills you with the urge to acquire the knowledge in order to claim the memory.

Mmm, could be, says Garret.

When she asked her father, he said that when he was in his teens, he went up to visit for a few weeks one summer, and formed a friendship with a girl there—my first girlfriend, he said, then added Maybe and made his daughter laugh—who subsequently wrote him letters in purple ink. He couldn't remember if the letters' contents reflected this startling, exotic and memorable quality. He remembered his Aunt Miriam getting annoyed at him, however, though he couldn't remember why. For being a teenaged boy, probably, he said. Something to do with that.

She tells all this to Garret as they lie on their backs in separate sleeping bags. Half the time he doesn't even say Mmm. Am I talking into a sponge? she asks. Nope, he says.

Beneath them is hard, rooted ground, while above, the night is clear. They are far enough from the mainland that the darkness is deep, the contrast with the sharp light of the stars heightened.

Garret's hand reaches out tentatively, travels across the ground to a place midway between them, and rests there. It is dark enough that she can imagine she doesn't see it. More, she thinks. Please. More.

Did you know, Lea continues, Great Aunt Miriam, Uncle

Byron's first wife, was known in the family and beyond—said my aunt, my father's sister—for being a looker, a real fashion plate. She came, or rather, stepped out, from Ottawa society. Now what would such a woman, this fashion plate, do in Peace River in the '20s and '30s? Were there, for example, any sidewalks for her to parade along? She must have been miserable.

In adult dress-up Lea has worn one of her flapper dresses, has felt the weight of the beadwork swing, swinging the fragile fabric sensuously against her bare skin. It made her want to dance. The dress is gone now. Given to a high school production of something, never to be seen again. She tries not to think of this. It angers her.

She vaguely recalls seeing Aunt Miriam when she and Uncle Byron moved to White Rock. The vision blurs if she concentrates too hard, looks at it too directly, so she approaches it slant. Aunt Miriam is a sick woman, a dying woman, in a great big bed with a frilly white bed spread. Lea feels uncomfortable because she is somewhere she does not belong, somewhere she doesn't know, and there is this heavy sombre sick smell in the air.

Have you ever seen anyone dying, or dead, Garret?

Yes. Not something I want to remember.

She reaches out her hand, but his is gone.

You are a pain in the ass, Garret, she says, before going on.

I know, he says.

On the other side of this island her great uncle lived with his second wife who, Lea has heard, was remarkably like the first. And addicted to mail order catalogues. This wife isn't even a blur, is just a dark spot of shadow where a person was. There is an accompanying sense that no one liked her, but the why is lost, if ever known.

Uncle Byron used old dental tools—buffers, files, picks, and pliers; a foot pump drill—to create lamps, plaques, boxes, all from juniper wood. In his boat he putted around to neighbouring islands and collected broken branches and driftwood for his projects. Lea has an egg cup at home. And a pencil holder. Uncle Byron swam every morning, year round, in the bay on which he lived, climbed down the steep steps to his dock. She remembers his aging chest heaving, his salty, wet old flesh, his satisfied smile and laboured breathing as he stood beside her putting his glasses back on.

She and her sisters slept in the Ark, a drydocked fishing boat with weeds grown high up its sides. Woke up to the sound of the sea, to the hard ribs and fixed wheel of the boat, to the security of solid land beneath the hull.

In the bay below the house, small islands like turtle backs disappeared when the tide came in in the evening. And then in the morning, they were back, fuzzy at first in the morning mist, then clear and solid. Isles of Enchantment. Magic.

Lea pauses. That's it. That's the story of my uncle.

Sounds great, says Garret. Thanks for telling me.

It was, says Lea. Now hold me, would you?

Garret is a small black blob far, far away, just moving out of her sight over a jutting clump of grey rock. Agile as an ant he clambers up, then down, and disappears.

She wishes she had come alone, and at the same time knows that she wouldn't be happier if she had. She's not good at being alone. She doesn't like to be alone in a house, hears things, checks locks too many times. She wonders from time to time if she will always have to live in a duplex or an apartment where she knows someone is within calling distance. Or with someone, a roommate or lover, or with a big dog. She envies women who are not troubled by solitude in this way.

When she is safe, she imagines herself alone in a cabin, imagines herself utterly self-reliant and therefore content. This always changes as nightfall and reality come or whoever is with her leaves. A part of her says it makes sense to be uneasy. Bad things do happen. But how, then, do other women do it? Live on an island, alone, an island like this one, with wind and cries of gulls for company, not fear. In a university class once a professor pointed out that if you fear, you are not free. She inevitably thinks of this in conjunction with being alone. And so maybe it is her need of Garret that irritates her, she thinks, more than he himself. That makes her abrupt, short-tempered.

She used to get that way with Phil.

There is a loneliness to Garret, a shellacked gentleness, which she has always found attractive. Something troubled, though not ominously so. She met him when someone brought him to a party she gave, and his interest in her fish tank was what gave them common, if not firm, ground for small talk. He seemed interested in everything she said, which was flattering. He was gorgeous to look at; tall and lanky, sinew more than muscle. And he was excruciatingly nice. And patient. Not many men put up with a schedule like hers, and if they did they usually filled what time there was with the sound of their own voices and the needs of their own bodies, as though she owed them for their patience.

But he's like a man turned into a hermit crab, she thinks. If she urges him, pokes him, he hides firmly inside. Only her kiss or touch draws him out and he kisses, touches, strokes back.

That night they pass a mickey of brandy back and forth as they watch the fire, poke it with pointed sticks, turn up the red hot bellies.

Garret, she says, this isn't going to work.

What isn't?

I'm sick of making the decisions all the time.

His eyes dart around and his hands hold each other. Not all the time, he objects.

Seems like. To me, anyway. I need someone else to make the passes once in a while. Pick the restaurants. Can't you do that? Couldn't you just try?

He stands up and moves his stool around to the other side of the fire.

Please talk to me, she says. Please?

He is silent for some time. Then he says, with a huge frustrated sigh, I guess I don't want to force you.

Neither do I, that's not what I mean.

I don't want you to do anything that you don't want to.

I won't, she says. Don't worry. I won't.

God, what's in his past? she wonders. She made her dog eat mud once. He bit her. She made her dolls sit up straight. What does he remember?

He's picking the label off the mickey.

Tell me? Please?

His eyes flicker with unhappiness and anger. Lea, I don't know who you think I am, but it sure as hell isn't me.

Oh Garret.

Garret is lying in the hot morning sun in his sleeping bag. Maybe he is dreaming he is going to hell, she thinks, watching his moist, red face. Or being clay-baked for cannibals. His face is flushed the way it is after sex.

They rent bikes in late morning and go all the way around the island, down every side road, up and down and around. She looks for her great uncle's driveway.

Was there a sign?

I don't know.

Was the driveway flat? Or did it go up or down?

I don't remember. It was bushy.

He sighs heavily. I'm just going to ride up this fork and

back. Check out the view. Talk to the plumber. Meet you
back here, okay?

She takes the lower fork and keeps looking, keeps catching
glimpses of the sea and tries to remember seeing a similar view
before. She loves her remembering; revels in it. Her memories
are as much a definition of herself as the present; she wouldn't
feel whole without them, would feel like a shadow. Her
warm, comforting memories are what give her texture.

She and Phillip drove down her uncle's woody, overgrown
drive in his 1969 Beaumont. Olive green with a black vinyl
roof. What made her want to visit her uncle? No idea now.
Phil. She was nuts about Phil for such a long time. Can still
see that loving look in his eyes. Why were they on the island
in the first place? Camping? Was it summer? Odd. Things
you assume you'll always remember. The speed bumps at the
A & W after you lost your virginities together. At Horseshoe
Bay pretending she was blind, he her guide, giving her
whispered descriptions of the pitying looks of passers-by. The
time down by the creek at her place, when they were lightly
stoned on organic mescaline, just enough to make the greens
so green, the sky so blue, the flowers many and bright, heaven
on earth and they were impossibly happy, madly in love
forever and ever. Oh I won't forget that, ever, you say,
supremely confident. So you don't bring the memories all the
way out to make sure they're still intact, and when years later
you do, the moths have been at them.

But they came to this island. That is for sure. A small cloud passes over the memory. She remembers that she left Phil in the car. Wait here, okay? She flushes, embarrassed at her younger self. At the time, she would have vehemently denied any suggestion that sometimes she was ashamed of him, but that appears to be true. Not when he was playing his Slingerland drums in his brother's band. No. When he played 'Wipeout,' there was nobody to compare with him except, maybe, Buddy Rich. Not when they cruised between the A & W and the Dog 'N Suds in his hot car with its mags and 396 engine.

Oh hell. Why do the bad parts come back? Phil waited in the car for a good hour.

What a little bitch.

He sat there waiting for her. Bending over backwards trying to please her. As always. Just wanted to be with her, that was all that mattered, he said. Such high praise, really. For which she had nothing but contempt.

His bike leans against the stop sign, and Garret is sitting under a tree with his head bowed. In his hands is a branch he is about to break in half. Beside him is a pile of broken sticks. Snap. She props her bike on its stand at the side of the road, and walks on mossy ground to join him.

How do you do. You must be Buddha, she says, smiling. Buddha building a fire.

He looks up at her with one eye closed against the sun and one hand shielding his face. The log he is sitting on is covered in moss. She sits down beside him, puts her arm around him.

Even as she sits he has begun to speak. He has dropped the pieces of broken branch and now his long arms tangle together like vines. He rushes, as though the faster he says the words the less he will feel them.

You keep pushing. Keep telling me to open up. Okay. I have to tell you something. Maybe it'll help. One of my happy memories. About Dad. Dear, dead Dad. Whenever I opened my mouth, he'd shut it. He made me feel stupid, that everything I said was stupid.

Garret reaches down, picks up half a stick. He snaps its branches into tiny pieces as he speaks, throws each bit onto the ground.

Garret—

Shut up. Shut up you stupid little turd. Who asked you, you stupid little shit.

Garret—

And so I have a bad time, okay? With talking. Offering ideas. I can't help it, Lea. I just can't help it. Like I said. I'm not Phillip the Wonderful or whoever the hell you think I am.

I never said you were! Oh Garret. I'm so sorry.

He stands up, knocking her hand out of the way just as it reaches towards him. I'm not very good at this, he says. Could I just meet you at camp, do you think? He is trembling from head to foot, putting on his sunglasses and starting towards his bike. Would that be okay?

Down at the beach, the tide is coming in. Hypnotic whoosh, whoosh as waves slap and lick around the rocks. Everything in the tidal pools will be washed over with cool salt water. How good that must feel, she thinks.

From her log she watches Garret, back down at the beach, but near. She watches him pick things up and feel them, drop them, or put them in his pocket. He is a good man. A kind man. She lies back against the warm rock and pretends to be seaweed. A bullwhip with slimy lasagna tresses; a sleek eel body. In warm water she slips around his calves, his thighs, his torso, his neck.

She pushed at Phillip until he broke, into heavy, pain-wracked tears. And then she left. Get it together, Phil.

Some things she'd rather forget.

Some things she'd better remember.

She imagines melting into the stone, adhering, becoming warm rock that, maybe, he would eventually approach to feel the texture of. She melts against the stone and the soft wax of her skin takes on its imprint. Touch me. Feel me. I'm soft and warm.

A wet anemone tongue, eel tongue, silvery barnacle tongue touches the skin between her heel and ankle bone. The pointed wetness moves with incredible slowness upward along her calf.

LOVELY
IN HER
BONES

INSIDE THE DOOR OF THE apartment stands the enormous china cabinet. Much of her mother's crystal, silver and china lives in here, behind the leaded glass. If you call that living, thinks Eleanor. Put to rest, more like it. None of it is ever used anymore, just dusted and polished. That tureen will never feel hot soup ladled in or out of it again; those paper-thin goblets will never chill and fog with lime sherbet; the three sterling serving dishes will never gleam and reflect flowers and people's faces at some family dinner. None will ever again rest on heavy linen tablecloths softened with silencers. Her mother is afraid to use everything. Except the flatware.

Why? Because it might get chipped, that's why. Or dented.

If you're careful, Mum, why not? No one would be more careful than us.

Don't argue with me. They are my things and if I want to protect them from mishandling—intentional or otherwise—that's my business.

Okay okay.

Many of Gramma's things went to Erin's condo. Purportedly for storage, but Eleanor knows better. Erin gets along with their mother, lives in a way she appreciates. They have the same shopping lists in life—Birk's, Larden's, Chalmers and Epcott—and the same Cross pens to check things off. If she isn't at home, Eleanor knows her mother is over at Erin's, checking out some new acquisition. She's been to Eleanor's exactly once.

If Eleanor is a little bitter about it, well she can't help it. Dregs are dregs are dregs. Who decides your life, anyway? Is it really just a series of lucky or unlucky guesses? What's the deal? Why didn't Erin marry a jerk who cancelled the insurance and burned the house down because she said she wouldn't go for a milkshake with him let alone ask him to move back in?

In the cabinet, too, way at the back on the second shelf, is a picture of Erin and Eleanor's dead father. In his air force uniform. He was killed in a training mission in the Arctic twenty-six years ago, right after Erin was born. He had come home only overnight, according to the family tale. Just long enough to see his new daughter, and to hug and kiss his wife and firstborn. When Eleanor is sleepy in bed, she thinks she remembers this night. Thinks she can remember his lips on her brow, his hand on her cheek.

Until lately, her mother has said she just can't bring herself to give nice things to Eleanor when she is living 'that way.' Has said, Your apartment is depressing, with its mildewed bathroom and fake grass carpet.

That doesn't mean I don't appreciate nice things, Mum.

I know that. I brought you up, remember? But sterling in a cellar? Your grandmother would be appalled.

Hello! I'm in the dining room! Eleanor follows a ribbon of White Shoulders down the hall. Her mother is seated at the table, well into her lunch. She seldom gets up to answer the door anymore; with her advancing arthritis, movements are often too painful. Each of her daughters has a key. Anyone else is evaluated from her chair, and dealt with by remote control.

Eleanor's mother wears a spright green dress that looks well with her white hair. It must be new; she likes to wear new things when people come to call. She is spearing an olive with a tiny silver fork. Her shaky hands compel her to chase it around her plate.

My but you're late. Did you let yourself in? I've started without you. I have a hair appointment this afternoon, you see. Drat this olive. No one's here. Perhaps I'll just pick it up. Pretend you don't notice, dear.

Sure. Nice dress, Mum.

Eleanor apologizes for being late, explains about the bus,

but her mother doesn't answer. Just glances at her rather sadly and spears another olive in a melancholy sort of way. Great start, thinks Eleanor.

The last time she was here, they had a big fight and she stomped off swearing never to return. She had asked her mother for money. Big mistake.

They were sitting in the living room. Across the room from each other. Eleanor was perched on a petit-point chair; her mother was, of course, on her chaise longue. They'd had tea, during which Eleanor had eaten too many cookies. Her mother was frowning. Eleanor figured there was nothing to lose. She was late with the rent and had received a written warning that morning from the landlady. So as she and her mother, together in the pale blue living room, sipped the last of the tea, she asked.

Mum? Could you possibly lend me some money?

Her mother smoothed her serviette in her lap.

Mum? I wouldn't ask if I weren't desperate.

The silence thickened like porridge.

Her mother, frowning more deeply, finally looked up.

Eleanor. When will you learn to manage your money?

Mum. . . . There's none to manage.

You must learn to make money make grow, said her mother. And launched into Lecture No. 1,711. Eleanor tuned out, stared at the begonias in their hanging baskets. Grow, she thought. Dimes thriving in full sun. Loonie bushes in rich soil. Tight wad heads of twos like cabbages peel them off.

Eleanor? I said, what about your rainy day fund? She paused with her head tilted, winked coyly.

Eleanor felt anger rising in her throat. Didn't she get it? Didn't she have a clue what *broke* meant?

Never be without a little something to fall back on. A little something. Remember that from *Winnie the Pooh*? How many times did I read that to you girls?

You read it to Erin, not to me. Mum, *please* listen! I have *nothing. Nothing!* And it's not my fault I haven't a goddamn cent.

Eleanor, please. You needn't resort to profanity to make your point. You always do.

How do you know that I always do *anything?* You don't know me at *all!* You're about as in touch with my life as—as *Dad* is. Tucked away back there in the goddamn china cabinet.

And she took the last cookie on the plate and stomped off. She'd pitch a circus tent in a field for the summer. Survive on dandelion leaves and fresh air.

Finally, her mother says, I'm glad you like the dress. It's new, you know. I'm not sure that I need it. But, well, here it is. Sit down. Please.

At Eleanor's place, on a Melmac plate, is a cheese sandwich. Velveeta on white. Sweet pickles on the side. Help yourself, says her mother.

Thank you, says Eleanor, as she sits down and picks up the sandwich. Mayonnaise drips like whitewash out the sides and glues the white bread to her teeth.

I don't usually have Velveeta around the house, you know. I got it in especially for you.

Thanks, Mum. Well. How have you been?

Oh, so so. I feel a little, I don't know, subdued these days. Maybe it's just my arthritis.

That's too bad. Are you . . .

Her mother waves away her words. Other people's woes are tiresome, I know. I know because I've heard enough of them myself. Let's see. Erin was here for lunch yesterday. We had a nice visit. She and Garnet are off to Germany soon; he has a convention. Erin is very excited; she likes to shop over there, she says. Maybe she'll get our Christmas presents over there; do you suppose? Christmas presents from Germany! Now wouldn't that be something. 'Santa Lucia.' Isn't she German? *Now 'neath the silver moon.* Remember?

A spasm of resentment jolts through Eleanor. Erin. Erin Erin. She tries to grab her next words back but can't. And did you have cheese sandwiches?

No. Asparagus. An asparagus quiche. Then she adds sharply, suspiciously, What do you mean by that?

Nothing.

Erin *brought* it. What is wrong with cheese sandwiches? You liked them well enough when you were growing up. Nothing I do seems to please you. You might do well to come down off your high horse. She stirs the pitcher of iced tea vigorously. The long glass spoon clangs against the pitcher like a warning bell. Tea? she asks. Tea?

Yes. Thank you. Eleanor silently chews, pensively eyeing her mother, and her mother's hair, which is flattened down on one side and wild on the other. It certainly does need doing. Talk about shock of white. Eleanor remembers the smell of hairspray—VO5—in the bathroom, tumbling out into the hall where she and her sister half pretended half truly choked on the smell and rolled around on the floor making gagging noises. Her mother steadily spraying the can, around and around her head, creating a chemical aura.

It's hard to believe she and her sister ever got along. Hard to believe they chased each other through the house, giggling and tickling. That Erin ever climbed up on the roof solely because it was bad. Or that Erin ever climbed a tree, let alone fell out of one, or slipped on the wet trunk of the log across the creek into nettles four feet tall—Eleanor had buckled over with laughter so hard she couldn't help Erin climb out. She still can laugh about it, though with considerably more malice now. Erin obscured by nettles except for her red playsuit and face. Later, Erin hot pink with calamine lotion, furious, swearing never to go into the woods again, at least not with her.

It isn't hard to believe, though, that Eleanor dropped a pop bottle down the chimney and blamed it on Erin.

Eleanor quite happily played alone in moss-laden nooks made by fallen trees. She drank water from the brook, nipped maple buds in the spring, and wished she were born an Indian.

Erin continued to dislike going outside. It isn't clean and

tidy out here; it isn't dustable or pressable. Her condo, for example, has no lawn or garden; it fills up its entire square footage with indoor 'living' space. Living space for people, not anything else. Not a plant in the place that Eleanor recalls. Mind you, she hasn't exactly frequented Erin's. Maybe a tasteful poinsettia at Christmas. A creamy lily at Easter. But that would be it. *She* might as well live in the goddamn china cabinet, too.

Erin. All Erin ever wanted to be was as socially graceful as their mother. So now she can sit back, fulfilled, for the rest of her life. While Eleanor feels like a huge, echoing void; hungers of all kinds gnaw at her insides, longings are constantly making her weep.

I *said,* how have *you* been, dear? Have you been looking for another place to live?

No.

Well, living the way you do, it's no wonder you're unhappy. Her mother is twisting her serviette now.

Mum?

Erin says that buying makes much more sense than renting, these days. You're not under anyone's thumb that way.

Mum!

I know. You don't want to take advice, particularly from Erin. I really don't know how the two of you got on such bad terms. It hurts me when you don't get along. It hasn't always been this way, I'm sure . . .

Hell. There's no point trying to interrupt when she's

being stubborn. Eleanor shuts out her voice, pretends to listen.

It's been almost six months since she saw Erin, spurting hairspray—pump now, not aerosol—in their mother's *en suite.*

You need some goals, Erin said then, speaking with held breath. And a good haircut.

You need some brains, said Eleanor.

Brains won't help you when you look the way you look; no employer, no man, is going to take a second look at you. Image is of vital importance, Eleanor, she said with the conviction of a fundamentalist. You look like a poor excuse for a man with that haircut. A man who doesn't have a proper barber.

Well, I guess you're entitled to your view of things.

Well I don't like to compare . . .

Then don't.

Fine.

You really don't like me, do you?

Oh no, Elly, that's not true. It's just that I'm not very *proud* of you, I guess.

You must learn to make money grow, her mother is saying. Again. And patting her hair in a distracted way. Then you can improve your circumstances. A peculiar look crosses her face then, and her voice trails off.

Mum? What is it?

Her mother is silent for almost a minute. She tilts her head slightly and looks faintly quizzical before she speaks. Nothing. Nothing much. And then she eases her chair back from the table, stands, moves slowly away and out into the middle of the room, where she seems cast adrift on blue wool rug.

Mum? What is it?

I don't know. You'll think it's silly. I don't know why, but out of the blue I just asked myself Why are you bothering to get your hair done? And I couldn't think of why. And that bothered me, somehow. She waves her hand. I'll be all right. Never mind. Oh I know. I know what I've forgotten. She turns and makes her way over to the chaise longue. Her arthritis, in her left hip, in both her hands, is indeed getting worse. Eleanor watches her sit, heavily, then reach down beside the chair to her black patent purse. She sets it on her knee. She tries to hide the trouble she is having undoing the clasp. Eleanor pretends not to see; she turns and stares out the patio doors at the city. Down at the speckles of people.

Her mother wails suddenly.

Eleanor spins around. Her mother is sobbing and wringing her hands.

I can't do it. I can't do anything any more with these horrible, useless things! I hate them!

The contents of her purse are tumbling to the floor, lipstick-smudged Kleenex, wallet, pen, cheque book, Tums, Renoir pill box.

A hot blade sears Eleanor's insides from heart to head.

Oh Mum. Let me help. It's okay. Eleanor sits beside her, goes to put her arm around her.

Her mother wrenches herself away. Just leave me be.

Eleanor gets up.

Mum—

I have to get to the bathroom. I have to fix my face. My hair. You are in the way.

Mum, here. Please let me help you.

No!

Eleanor's mother stands up slowly and takes one step forward. But she steps onto her compact, which slips; she is going to fall. She reaches out and grasps Eleanor, who is still standing right beside her. Eleanor steadies her mother, supports her while she regains her composure. Eleanor can smell the traces of VO5, of White Shoulders, but pervading these is the unique scent of her mother. As she holds her, firmly, close, she can feel her mother's china bones through her thinning flesh. How frail her mother is getting to be.

WATERS
OF THE
HEART

ON HER WAY THROUGH
Williams Lake, Leslie stops to visit an old friend. An old best
friend, actually, from seven to twenty-one, and then Carmen
moved up country, Leslie to Edmonton.

During these reunions, every year or two, tradition has had
them get pretty loaded, to break the ice, to mellow things
out. Pissed up laughing and crying and hugging and parting.
But times and things have changed. Leslie quit liquor and pot
a year ago. She's somewhat apprehensive about there being
no buffer zone between them; it won't be much fun for
Carmen. She'll be disappointed in her. Leslie can imagine her
reaction: Jesus Christ, Les. You're no fun any more, are you?

When they were little, Leslie wanted them to be twins, but

she betrayed herself and grew taller. And her dark brown hair stayed straight and silky, Carmen's curly and blonde. Through elementary school they were the only girls in their grade. They never played with anyone else. They were going to have a riding school in England when they were twenty. Twenty. When life would be in order and all would be well. Twenty. When the smooth sailing began. At recess and lunches they were horses in a ring, whinnying and skittish, shying away from jumps and soaring over them, mincing over cavalettis and holding their Arabian heads high.

Carmen lived a quarter mile from the school, and Leslie would stand in the schoolyard waiting for her to start down the hill on her bike. Leslie remembers her autumn-leaf-coloured parka the best, with its fuzzy trim around the big hood. Remembers the day it was brand new. Sometimes Carmen's mother had pinned a towel around her neck, for her swollen glands. Once a year she came late, with an ash cross on her forehead. If she didn't come, if she was sick, the day at school was long and boring. All day Leslie hoped she was just late, maybe with some church thing. She was restless, distracted; she didn't want to do anything, to learn anything, that might make them unequal in any way.

They had '63 vw's when they were seventeen, went on long country drives toking Thai stick and drinking off-sales beer, playing movie camera on the hilly dark country roads. After high school Carmen worked for a doctor for a while, and then in a drinking straw factory. Leslie stayed home and stared out the window wondering what she wanted to do. Eventually she got on at the A & W. Carmen and Ben, one of her boyfriends at the time, would come in to say hi after the drive-in got out, offer her tokes and swigs of beer in the back corner of the lot. One night a buddy of his, Randy, came along, and they all went for a drive when she got off work. Things worked out and the four of them started going out together. Driving into Vancouver for concerts, over to the Cloverdale Hotel where their ID worked, sometimes to White Rock for a walk along the pier and a beer at the O.B.

Eight-track tapes filled the front seat of the G.T.O., beer bottles the back. Ben drove at about eighty everywhere they went, and they whooped and hollered and threw empties at road signs. Randy and Ben were a gas, even though now she can't remember a thing they said. Leslie was sure she was in love with Randy. He was so funny. And when he and Carmen started joking around like Cheech and Chong, you'd bust a gut from laughing.

Carmen always had all the boys after her. Went through them like draft beer. Because she was more desirable, Leslie assumed. Because she was prettier, sexier, funnier.

Carmen married for the first time and moved up country. Had her first baby. Leslie went east. Drank and smoked too much, worked in bars and lounges, didn't marry or even come close, eventually went back to school and has been there ever since, seven, eight years now, lusting after myriad subjects and professors, living more in her head than out of it. For her it was the loneliness that got her in the end. The utter loneliness of coming back to where she lived to nobody and nothing and the slow dawning realization that her whole life would consist of just this and worse if she didn't do something to change it. Books and drinks and failed, embarrassing, encounters which were failed and embarrassing because she wanted to be like Carmen when she was drunk, vivacious and cute, but instead she was incoherent, slow, and sleepy.

If Carmen's house reflects the state of her mind, then she is going through some wild and troubled times. Stuff strewn all over, good stuff bad stuff clean stuff dirty stuff. Bags bottles orange peels and apple cores. Outdoor dirt in the bathtub, bleach in the toilet. Clothes and dishes and toys and papers on and under everything. Havoc. Her children are with their fathers this weekend. Hallelujah.

I quit three months ago myself, Carmen says, pouring coffees. Drinking. Dope. All the fun things. Quit or die, Les. That's what it is.

I know, Leslie answers.

Life cannot go on like this is what I realized, says Carmen, fingers moving constantly, smoothing, picking, flexing, flicking. My life cannot go on like this. The stuff I thought was saving me is actually trying to kill me.

It gets better. I'm proud of you.

Goddamn hard. Having to look at all the crap in my swamp.

Alligators and tse-tse flies.

You name it. It's in this fat head somewhere.

I know what you mean.

For the first time they don't start in a haze and regress into thoughts awash, saturated, with memory. They are in the clear-eyed present, and the fuzzy past is something they have escaped from with their lives.

So much I forgot about, Carmen says. So many rotten things I did that are just working their way through the fog now. God they're ugly up close. Deformed kittens I'd like to drown. You know? I'm sure sorry about a lot of them. But what can I do about what I've already done? I bet there are things with you, too, that I've forgotten. Times I was rotten. Are there?

I've forgotten a lot too. But yes. There are a couple of things I remember. That I wish I didn't. Things that made me sad.

Like what?

I don't know that I want to talk about them.

You have to tell me so I can deal with them.

They don't all have to do with you.

Just the ones that do, then.

Leslie takes a deep breath and says, Okay. You asked for it. Then she looks steadily at Carmen, changes her mind, and says, I'm always kind of pissed off, whenever I see you. But I still want to see you.

Okay. Carmen lights a cigarette off the end of another.

I guess I'm angry at you because for all these years I have kept us in contact, and I know it isn't very close or reliable contact. But I've always sent birthday cards, Christmas cards. How many have you sent me? One Christmas card. One Christmas card when you married Paul and decided to be a good Catholic wife and mother for a while. So even that wasn't a personal gesture. Not really.

Is that it?

No. I . . . I've always suspected that you make fun of me behind my back the way I've heard you make fun of other people. I don't think I'm special to you the way you are to me. This year for the first time I almost didn't send you a card. But I did. You used to be my best friend. I don't think I was ever yours.

As she speaks she feels herself standing in the schoolyard of Wrengate School at recess or lunch hour, feeling left out of a game and hurt. She feels childish and whiny, doesn't like herself. Why don't you like me? What's the matter with me? Her adult self saying Just forget it, forget it, but the present child is too strong.

Is that it?

—

What else?

Nothing.

What else?

Nothing, I said.

Okay, Carmen says. My turn. I've started to realize a lot of things, Leslie, she says, trying to smile, eyes filled with tears. Like how I've taken an awful lot of people for granted over the years. I'm trying to do better. I really am. I love you, you know. I really do. I'm sorry.

Well don't get mad if I say I'll believe it when I see a letter in my mailbox. Deal?

Deal.

They hug and kiss and Leslie feels anger, and love, and hurt. Surging up her throat, vile waves wanting to surface, wanting to be told, and she pushes away, down, back, again and again. Until it stays back. She smiles and waves as she pulls out of the driveway. Blows a kiss.

West of Prince George, in a forest, a car ahead of Leslie pulls off the side of the road. The back door opens, and a large, elderly woman empties onto the road three McDonald's milkshake cups, a folded up disposable diaper, and two ashtrays, one from the front seat, one from the back.

Leslie sees this as she pulls up behind them and around to pass. It is too late to stop, but she imagines, once she realizes what they are doing, slamming on the brakes and yelling at them. Out in the middle of nowhere, alongside the mighty undrinkable unfishable Fraser River. Amid logged hillsides that look like the shaved skin of diseased dogs. Beautiful B.C. Do your part. Bastards.

She spends the next hour thinking about them. Plotting revenge. She imagines pasting a sticker that reads I LITTER on their trunk when they are stopped for coffee somewhere. She imagines a scene in a coffee shop when she confronts them. The waitress is pouring their coffee. They are all lighting cigarettes. Leslie stands to one side and waits. When the waitress moves away, she moves in. She says loudly (she practices the words on Brie, her dog, up beside her on the passenger seat; he looks appropriately dismayed at the anger in her voice, and she feeds him cookies from her pocket in

71

between tries) I saw you pull over to the side of the road with the intent to litter. I saw you dump your garbage on our highway. It is illegal to litter. I think what you have done is terrible, and I hope something awful happens to you. Goodbye.

There is not a coffee shop ahead.

There are things, she says to Brie, over which we have no power. Brie pants and turns his head towards the window.

The campground office smells like Christmas dinner at four in the afternoon.

I put you near this building, the Spanish-speaking woman says. You be safe that way. Okay?

I'll be safe, she answers. I have a big dog.

The woman is big like a bean bag chair, and slow. As they speak, her husband comes heavily down the stairs to the ringing phone. Now he is on his way out the door. He nods at Leslie. The screen door slams behind him. The woman looks crestfallen. I cooked a turkey dinner she says, and look! He no have time to finish.

Bastard, thinks Leslie.

There is no one else in the campground. Her campsite is speckled with last year's cigarette butts. The water in the outdoor taps has not yet been turned on for the season. Brie refuses Perrier. She fills his dish in the bathroom. There is a sign on the door: CLOSED FOR CLEANING BETWEEN 1 AND 12. Posted in each shower stall is a small sign: NO SHOES IN THE SHOWER, PLEASE.

The water in the swimming pool is smooth and still. When she sits on the edge of the pool, her toes, feet, calves disturb the surface, send ripples and echoes through the room. She stops moving, sits silent waiting for sound to cease. Then she slides in and breast strokes up and down. Once. Swims around the four corners in one direction and then the other. Diagonally across both ways. On her front, on her back, on her side. She and only she makes the watery echo sounds in the silence and gloomy light of the pool room, only her body causes the texture and timbre of the water to change, and she feels it lap against her skin.

Carmen.

When Carmen and Leslie were nineteen, Randy and Ben took them over to Victoria for the weekend. At the Red Lion they drank two tables of beer. The guys shot some pool, they listened to the band, danced a bit. Everything was cool. But when they got back to the motel, Carmen and Leslie's boyfriend went into a room and wouldn't come out. Wouldn't answer knocks, wouldn't answer phone calls. Leslie and Carmen's boyfriend stared glumly at each other and at Johnny Carson. Carmen's boyfriend came over and sat beside her on the orange and red bedspread, handed her a beer and said, Well, we may as well even the score. No, said Leslie, to both. No thank you. She slept in the bathtub and tried to imagine. And couldn't. Couldn't believe that either of them would really do this to her. Couldn't imagine that she could matter so little to Carmen. She lay there in that empty dripping tub, drunk as hell and sick at heart, trying, trying to make sense, make sense without pain, of what was happening.

She turns and kicks off the end of the pool with both feet, hard. Glides as far as she can before breaking the surface for air. Her lungs hurt. The waters are clearer in this memory than in most others. Oh God Betrayal. The dismay wells up, the It must have been a mistake, the She wasn't reading it right, It couldn't really have happened. Too cruel a thing for a best friend to do. Carmen never said a word.

How could you how could you. How could you do this to me.

If she had brought it up, would Carmen have even known why? Or would she have just looked at her with that slight sneer and said *Jeez*us, Les, who the hell cares?

Or she might not remember. Utterly inconsequential. Just sex. Just another guy. Just another night.

Up and down, up and down the pool she swims, the water stroking her, stroking her.

What are friends for? She had thought that they defined, complemented, even constituted each other, and that long time, long long time together, confirmed that. She had refused to see, let alone welcome, difference. In retrospect, suddenly, she sees herself as the hanger-on, the doormat, the fool who defined friendship in terms of—yawn—loyalty and trust and admiration. Her terms. Not Carmen's. No idea, now, gloomily, cynically, what the criteria were on which Carmen based their friendship. Habit?

Up and down thrice more, with ferocious turns. Then she lies on her back in the settling water. Her head stays floating while the rest of her slowly sinks.

If you met her right now you wouldn't be friends in a million years, she thinks, as her feet touch bottom.

Two powerful kicks and she is at the side of the pool. She hoists herself out and stands dripping on the edge.

Leslie and Brie walk through the empty campground to the bush on the other side.

You know, she didn't say a goddamn word about what I've been through, Brie. Didn't say I'm proud of you. Didn't ask a goddamn thing. Nothing. Me me fucking me. Chump. Sucker. Eh Brie? Your mother's a twit. Did you know that? A fucking twit. She'll never write.

Brie wags and pants and pulls on the lead. She lets him go and he is away like a shot. Leaps over a log like a show horse, ears perked forward, front legs tucked under.

She stands on the edge of the woods and closes her eyes. She hears the wind begin. She has forgotten that it begins, comes out of stillness. It has been a long time since she heard it. Now she hears it whisper, mutter, rustle through the leaves both individually and all at once. A sweeping rustle of wind through the trees.

She can't remember when last she heard the wind. At home children yelling, and cars sizzling by, muffled and masked wind. It is action, not sound, unless it howls. Wind does, not sounds. In a quiet world you can hear its ebb and flow.

There is rhythm involved. Out of silence and stillness comes the start of a tender crescendo, a pianissimo hush of sound, moving, moving, stirring, stirred. Growing. Shhshh sounds, yes. But much taller, and narrow for each tree, and broad-reaching.

Brie comes back. He licks her hand and stands, still, beside her, listening too.

It is silent in the campground at night. Replete with trees and quiet. Not even big trucks passing. Deep sleep, rock sleep. Brie is curled like a man against the side of her sleeping bag.

In very early grey morning, Brie growls. Shoves his nose through the fly window, growls louder. Leslie lies still and tense. Waits. Then Brie lies back down and curls up again. They sleep.

In the morning she reaches down and throws the breaker. The electric heater and the coffee maker come on. She and her dog lie dozing until the coffee machine sputters and the van is warm. Good dog. And out the door he goes. Tearing after smells and squirrels, running deep into the empty campground, under tipped up picnic tables, around water taps with their big lying signs: WATER.

ERGOT

M<small>Y</small> MOTHER STANDS with her back to me, looking out the hospital window, gently stroking her cheek with her hand as she speaks; it is a gesture of self-comfort, I think. From my antiseptic green and white bed I stare hard at this back, this back of a person I have been angered by so often, this person I have claimed to hate, off and on, for so many years. I want to look hard at her. I want to really see her. But if I looked this hard at her front, into her face, her eyes, it would make her, and me, terribly uncomfortable. After all, who taught me that it is rude to stare? So I look at her back. At the pinks and turquoises in the weave of her Irish woollen suit. Her shoulders aren't as square as mine. She is shorter than I am. Her hair is greying but still not half-way grey even though she is in her seventies.

The hand that strokes her cheek is gnarled and freckled. I like the freckles, though she doesn't. Age spots, she calls them. I see her favourite ring, my grandmother's aquamarine with its circlet of diamonds, on her nobbly hand. I have always wondered how she can wear rings, if her hands are as ugly as she says they are. You will never have nice hands, she said to me once. Not with the hands on both sides of your family.

I have never worn rings. I used to try to eat my hands, nails first. Now I hold them in my lap, under the table cloth, under my sweater, and when I'm alone I stare at them and try to see how they differ from other people's, but so sure I am of their tremendous ugliness that I cannot judge them objectively. I've considered taking a picture of them. Then I could hang it on the wall and stand far back from it and look. I've never got around to this project.

When my mother had her hysterectomy, I was fifteen. I went to visit her in the hospital, but I wanted to leave the whole time. To get out to the parking lot and my boyfriend, where he sat waiting, listening to the Moody Blues. *On The Threshold of a Dream.* Smoking cigarettes. I thought of his flat belly and the way he flicked his reddish blonde hair back off his eyes. I pictured how his freckled hands rested on the steering wheel, how one slid between my thighs. For the first time in my life I was in love. Someone had seen my breasts and between my legs. Nothing else mattered.

At home there had been, for weeks, a peculiar bloody smell and a crazy woman. I thought with horror of something decaying and rotten. Our house the House of Usher sinking into a swamp. Fracturing like a vase and crumbling into putrid water. My mother angry all the time, crying, screaming. I was out with Ian whenever I could. Take me out. Take me away.

Hysterectomy. This the end then of the soaked, bloody napkins, the smell, the screaming and crying. Fear and loathing. Sickness unto death. I hated her. I hated her smell.

My mother turns back to me. Frances Sinclair Smith, she says. That's it. Frances Sinclair Smith. He had been through the Great War before he came to Canada.

Mum, what has he got to do with Gramma?

She has been telling me tales of my grandparents, of her childhood in the '20s in Calgary, things I've never heard before. I am particularly interested in my grandmother. She has always been peripheral, a distant connection. Certainly no part of my life. A photograph, mainly, that used to sit on my mother's dressing table, amongst silver rouge and powder boxes, perfume bottles. Gramma with netting over her face; Gramma with eyes that glanced, softly darted, eyes that touched edges, not centres. A romantically blurred figure, her pale hands folded in her lap.

You'll see. Be patient—you could use some practice. When I was a little girl, Frances Sinclair Smith came to Alberta. He came from England to be a rancher, and settled in Millarville. He brought his old nursemaid with him. To keep house. Now she was a character. What he would have done without her, I really don't know. Good natured, though her voice was perhaps a little loud for who she was. Anyway. I'm getting ahead of myself. For a number of years he tried to grow crops. Things just didn't work out. Early frosts, droughts, too much rain. But one summer, finally, the grain grew green and beautiful and high, and seeded out. Our family drove out on a Sunday to visit. Your Aunt Lydia, and I, and our parents. A hailstorm wiped out the crop just before we arrived. I remember the sound the hail made on the car. I remember driving into his yard and seeing the hail deep on the ground. It crunched under the tires. And the air smelled so clean. And oh oh. Seeing Frances Sinclair Smith sitting at the kitchen table weeping was the saddest thing I ever saw.

There is a long pause.

And that's it? I say.

That nursemaid, she says. I can't remember her name. But she came up behind him at the kitchen table and put both of her big wide hands on his shoulders. Buck up, she said. Buck up there, Master Smith, it isn't the end of the world. We were standing outside; we could hear her through the opened window. Frances Sinclair Smith lifted his head and rested his cheek on her wide, capable hand. I can see it to this day. His red face; her white hand. You know, if it weren't for her, I think he would have packed up and gone then and there. The experience would have broken him. If it weren't for her.

She looks far out the window for a long time. Then she says, There have been some strong women in this world, Claire.

Like you, I say.

And you, she says.

There is another long pause.

Gramma? I say softly.

Gramma. Well yes, her too. In her way. Oh you want the rest of the *story*. All right. One week, later, maybe even years later, the nurse—she was an Englishwoman, by the way—came into town to do some shopping, and she stopped by our house to deliver a message. She was very flattered that my mother asked her to stay for a cup of tea, and not in the kitchen, either. I was in my favourite place, hiding under the piano. The maid brought everything in, and with it mother's medication. The nurse saw the medication and, midway through a scone, asked carefully, And how long have you been taking this? Several months, said mother. Months! cried the woman, standing right up. Months! You must stop *right now!* She held out her hand like a school teacher and your poor startled grandmother meekly passed over the medicine.

No wonder she—your grandmother—went a little funny in the head, I suppose. Ergot is poisonous if you take it too long. Her fingers were very pale, I remember. The nurse held them in her hands. Like minnows, she said. Like little poisoned minnows.

Yikes, I say. What's ergot?

Ergot is a fungus. A disease on cereal grasses. Did they give it to you? To stop the bleeding?

No. There must be something else now.

Yesterday I woke up in a blood-soaked bed. Bleeding and

bleeding and bleeding. I thought I was going to die. I called my mother and lay back in terror.

My mother, still turned away, says, When my mother was in the hospital, I wasn't allowed to visit. This is before the ergot.

Why was she in hospital?

A tumour. She had a tumour removed.

Where?

In her stomach. My mother, she says, shivering, bending over slightly as though she has a pain, had a nine-pound tumour removed from her stomach.

God.

She was rather unwell ever after.

I would say so.

She turns around and our eyes meet, briefly. Then she turns away. Her unwillingness to share herself and her emotions with me is a constant reminder of what true Victorians my grandparents were: emotions are for suppressing, not expressing. I have often felt unloved, and it occurs to me that she may have felt the same. May feel the same even now. By me? Propriety. The alternative is disgusting chaos.

I suddenly remember visiting my grandmother in the nursing home. One time she lifted up her nightgown. I want to show you my scar, she said. I didn't know what kind of scar. I thought maybe on her leg. I didn't say no. It was rude to say no. It is polite to appear interested. Be nice to your grandmother. I saw long grey pubic hair and wrinkly pale flesh. I was sickened and afraid. My mother stepped in front of me and pulled the nightgown down. Stop it mother. Stop it right now. That must have been this scar.

My grandmother was quite unhinged by then. My grandfather was dead and, out of kindness to her—must have been, surely, in some incomprehensible way—he had put in his will that the house was to be disposed of immediately. So the house was sold from under her. She didn't last in the apartment. She went wandering at odd hours, seeking.

I've got to go for a while, says my mother. She pulls on her turquoise leather gloves. I have some errands to run.

Okay, I say, and lie back. I want to sleep. It feels forever since I have been by myself.

My sister and I played Frankie and Johnnie on our grandparents' garden swing. We picked gooseberries and currants alongside their house on Montcalm Crescent. That was the summer before the November that he died, the summer before the late spring she went from apartment to nursing home. We were visiting, with our white Ford Falcon station wagon and our trailer. I left my furry pink teddy under the bed and wrote asking my grandmother to send him.

I think about the nine-pound tumour. Such a hole. Such a gaping emptiness.

And where was my grandfather in this round of trouble? A shadow on the margins of Women's Troubles. Importune for him to ask, importune for her to tell him.

I sleep, and think I am having a baby. My orange belly

inflates as I watch myself in the mirror. I feel my internal organs pushed out of the way. I feel my breathing restricted from pressure on my diaphragm. I get bigger and bigger and bigger. I feel doubt. I am not sure I want a baby. I cannot remember an act leading to conception. But there is a room in my house filled with baby things. I must want it, I decide. Then I go to a concert at the Queen Elizabeth Theatre, something with chamber music, and at intermission I go home.

I know my baby is a she. I talk to her, sing to her on the bus. Tap rhythms with all ten fingers on my huge stomach. Her name is Coralie.

The baby I have when I get home is not a baby. It is a nine-pound cyst, a nine-pound lump of scar tissue slimy with my blood, a hard rubbery dolphin mass slippery white and red.

When I wake up the first thing I see is my mother's crooked hands. They smooth the wool up the sides of her lap and back again, slowly, slowly. I remember her setting the table with this gesture; the silencer, then the cloth, her sure and competent hands smoothing, smoothing, before placing the silver. She stroked the horse like this too. Smooth down his nose and the velvety spots on either side, smooth down his foreleg, around the curve of his flank. And tucked her plants into earth in the same way. Soft pressure to tamp the earth around the roots, light touch to dust bits of earth from the leaves.

Mum, I was so awful. When you had your hysterectomy. I'm sorry for being so selfish.

You came to visit me.

But I was rude and just wanted to go the whole time. I wasn't very nice.

That was a long time ago now.

Fifteen to thirty-six.

That's a long time ago.

Yes. Three sevens.

Well then.

Now my mother is holding her hands out and looking at them, at their short, pointed nails, at their arthritic knuckles. I think of ancient sea turtles. She lowers them and smoothes her lap again.

Did Grandpa love her?

Oh I'm sure he did. In his own way. He got a little tired of her ill health after a while, I think. It did go on.

His own way, I think but do not say. What good is loving in your own way if it isn't the way of the person being loved? What good can it do if the recipient cannot feel it, hear it, if the love is a flower in a lead box?

Mum? Will you come closer so I can kiss you?

She looks a little embarrassed. But after a moment she comes over to my bed.

You will feel better when all this is over and you can go home, she says. My, you look pale.

She smoothes my hair, brushes it off my face. Her gnarled

hands touch my temples, stroke my cheeks. She pats my hands and I take hers in mine. I look at them together.

Mum? Did Gramma have hands like ours?

Yes she did. And she didn't like them any more than we do. You should have seen her glove collection.

And she bends to kiss me.

THE RAIN
IN SPAIN

IN THE SUMMER BETWEEN grades ten and eleven, Dwight's daughter Rebecca met a long-haired nobody with blond hair in his eyes, a rat-tail comb in his pocket, and a loud fast car. His pants were so tight he'd likely become sterile. He wore black, scuffed ankle boots with pointed toes, and had a cigarette pack tucked under the sleeve of his t-shirt. Now you're getting somewhere, Dwight told her. Now you're really moving along. Take him to a dance at your school why don't you?

Don't judge people by appearances, Dad.

Dwight's wife, Mary, prodded him, said, You've got to do something about this, Dwight. Rebecca won't have anything to do with me. She's in that phase where she hates her mother. And Dwight? Staring out the window isn't going to help.

Neither is staying at the office. Consider this your big test, Dwight. Get involved in your daughter's life now or it's going to be too late. In more ways than one.

Dwight stared out the window and ignored Mary. He ignored the boy, too, hoping he would somehow just go away. No such luck. The summer was tense and long, and virtually silent, except for the '67 Mustang roaring up and down their driveway.

It was with a huge sigh of relief that Dwight dropped Rebecca at the ferry in September. Looking so correct and tidy in the box-pleated grey skirt, the grey dress blazer, the royal blue knee socks and black oxfords. And he heaved another big sigh, but this time of dismay, when, three months later, he received the call that said she was gone. Had run away. Back here, no doubt, to find that useless fellow, damn him anyway.

Mary had no comment when Rebecca ran away from school, no suggestions on what to do, because she herself was gone by then. You want silence, Dwight? she said. All right. I give.

In the November days of endless rain, Dwight chopped wood and made himself huge fires in the fireplace, sat staring at the leaping flames, and thought of cowboys and branding irons and *Iron John*, which he hadn't read but had heard of and had recommended to several of his male patients. Fires had been forbidden while Mary was here. She didn't like the dirty grate, didn't like the fire itself which was once, he argued, one of the big three of human survival. A gas fire would do just as nicely and help save the environment, she said. No, he said. A gas fire isn't authentic. Look at yourself, she retorted. And get these bits of wood off the rug.

At Christmas time Lenny the dog was the only creature at home. *He* was always glad to see Dwight. Because he was hungry, Dwight suspected on gloomy days, not because he loved him. Other times he thought maybe Lenny did love him, times when the black dog leapt into his lap and licked his hands. Unsanitary as he knew it to be, Dwight bowed his head and kissed Lenny the dog on the bridge of his nose.

Dwight had no idea where Mary was. She hadn't told him. And his daughter stayed at the boy's house, with the boy's parents, and called to say Merry Christmas in a somewhat fearful and questioning way. What kind of people these were to harbour her thus was a good question, but one he was incapable of approaching at that point. Here his wife had wrenched herself out of his life; that in itself was almost more than he could bear. He was like a severe burn case, he decided; so much burned flesh and pain that all he could do was lie as still as possible and keep himself anaesthetized. Objectivity was impossible; decisions were impossible. He remained immobile, distant, for over a month. Spent no more than three hours a day at the office and wasn't much use, he suspected, when he was there. He made a lot of referrals. Wanted only to stay at home and pet the dog, watch the fire, stare out the windows.

Mary called one day to hear about Lenny. How was he? He's just had open heart surgery, Dwight said. Oh, and his hip has been replaced. But we're doing fine. We're mending. After my operation, I'm a little—well, you don't want to hear about me. How is your new life? How is the city? Are you on English Bay? I'm sure it suits you.

He knew very little about what suited her, she said, which was why she left. And she was in Freeport, not Vancouver. Why the hell couldn't he have worked less when she and Rebecca were there? That would have made all the difference. Maybe. He knew nothing much about them at all. Talk about closing the gate when the horses are gone. Or opening it, actually, she added. And why wasn't Rebecca home yet? What was she doing? Why didn't he know? Never mind. She knew where Rebecca was. Had even tried to call, but Rebecca hung up on her. Still in that phase. What kind of a father was he? As a matter of fact, I'm taking her to Europe, Dwight said suddenly. Well that's something, Mary said. Really something. There was a long pause. Then she said, I still love you, by the way. Then there was another long pause. Keep in touch, she said finally, knowing he couldn't. Ta ta, she added, because it pissed him off. Then she hung up. He stood beside the telephone table, holding the receiver tight against his chest, until an operator's voice ordered him to hang up and try his call again.

In the middle of a January night Rebecca called and in a waif's voice said she was very very sick. Would he come and get her, if she gave him the address? Off he went to the despised location, and bundled his child into the car and home where, he hoped, she would now stay. The sickness was just stomach flu. She was fine in a day or two, and, lo and behold, she didn't leave.

What exactly kept her there he wasn't sure. She didn't offer explanation—she wasn't a talker at the best of times, and he didn't want to push her. He never saw her. She was usually gone except when she slept, which was late into the morning. When he came home at lunch time, the smell of fresh cigarette smoke might tell him she had lately risen and left. But it soothed him just knowing that someone else was home sometimes, considered this home. It reassured him that the family was not disintegrated completely. Geographically, anyway. His daughter was back at home. That was a beginning.

He didn't charge her rent, because if he did, he decided, she would leave again. And she wouldn't go back to school, private or public. Until September, she said. So he settled on requiring that she get a job. He couldn't demand that she stop seeing the boy, Darren was his name, for that too might make her leave. It seemed his parents would keep their door open for her, she said. She could always go back and be their daughter, she told him, since they didn't have one. Well isn't that nice, he murmured. Such nice people.

Dad—

Do something really nice for her, said Sasha, his office nurse. Guilt can pack a wallop. Now there was a woman who could, he supposed, love him, but that was no good because he loved his wife, and that was all the heartache he needed. Sasha was full of bright ideas. About the office, his life (which included his daughter, but not his wife). About the things they could do if he would let her farther into his life outside work. The latter she hinted at in such a way that he was able to pretend not to notice. Which was generous of her. Maybe Rebecca will feel obligated, said Sasha. Maybe she'll feel grateful. Maybe it will change her life.

Maybe, he said. Maybe. And his lie to Mary about Europe came to mind.

There was nothing he could do about his wife by now, but a trip might straighten Rebecca out. It might show her there was more to life than the Dog 'N Suds, where she was currently working. The drive-in wasn't quite what he had had in mind. Drive-in restaurants were like drive-in theatres, to his mind: suspect in every regard. Habitués of one were habitués of the other, and both were Bad News; both encouraged a kind of drive-in approach to life. Completely unacceptable. As well, a trip to Europe would get her away from her boyfriend, which couldn't be anything but good.

He steeled himself and drove to the Dog 'N Suds. He parked as far down the covered walkway as he could without being off the parking lot and in the ditch. It would be clear to any who cared to notice that he was only marginally there, not truly, not voluntarily, not happily.

He could see his daughter inside behind the huge glass panels. Customers were not allowed in there, a sign said; only the car hops and cooks. Lunch was over, pretty well. There were only four other cars in the lot, and only two of them souped up. The boy's wasn't there. So every waking minute wasn't spent with him. His daughter was inside, playing with her change maker and talking to another carhop. He saw the girl give his daughter a nudge, and she turned. When she saw him, his car first, then him, a look of astonishment took over her usually expressionless face. When she was small, her face was like this, he remembered—in constant, vibrant motion. Then she came out the door and the mask went back on as she walked towards him under the canopy, along the concrete. He could hear the shake of the coins in the dispenser around her waist as she walked. Her black pants had a yellow stripe up the side, like a mountie's pants, and she wore a little jacket of the same yellow stuff, and a white blouse and tie. Pretty, slender, brittle girl with shoulder length brown hair and bangs. With eyes which should more truly be called hazel—medium brown with gold flecks. With such a solemn face.

Geez hi Dad, she said. What can I get you?

He felt nervous, as though he were asking her on a date. Well a root beer would be fine.

Large or regular?

It doesn't matter. Either would be fine. Medium.

Okay.

And away she went. His nervousness temporarily subsided, replaced by the more consistent displeasure he took from this place. Everything about it made him want to leave. It was threatening, though there was no one here, though the weather was fine, the asphalt and concrete swept, the glass windows clean, the uniforms not provocative or suggestive in any way.

Roll up you window halfway, Dad, she said, or the tray will fall off.

She immediately agreed to go. Europe was, after all, the thing for young people to do. Three weeks in Spain. The only drag would be having her father along, he supposed.

Far out, she said. Sure, she said. Then, I don't have any money.

Well I have some, he said. But you will have to provide your own spending money.

Okay, she said. Geez. Europe. Spain. Far out. I'd kiss you, Dad, but I'd knock the tray off.

Because of his rising spirits, he wanted to make some snide comment, say, How on earth will you survive without that greaseball for three weeks, but he didn't. What if she changed her mind? Besides, a car pulled into her section, a beat-up old station wagon containing a woman and three children, and turned on its lights. Her signal to go.

He still saw very little of her until just before the trip—he left her notes from Sasha about her passport and so on. It was like arranging a holiday with a penpal. A new penpal you didn't yet know at all, except from the picture.

Dwight's brother Vic would look after Lenny while they were gone, because Lenny hated the vet and the kennel. Vic or his wife would go to the house each day to feed the dog and give him a pat. Maybe one night the two of them would go and watch TV there. The night before the trip, Dwight and Rebecca loaded their luggage into Vic's car, while Lenny was asleep by the fire. Their whispering and bumbling secrecy for the sake of the dog brought giggles, and for a brief moment there was almost a connection, Dwight thought, an omen, he hoped, for the trip. But at the airport next day, there was the boy to see her off, aloof, smoking, and she ignored her father until they had to board the plane.

Wherever they were—Madrid, Toledo, Seville, Malaga— she wrote letters to the boy. (He does have a name, Dad. His name is Darren, and I happen to be in love with him.) In Cordoba he saw the start of one, before she snatched it from under his nose with a filthy look: Oh dear Honey Bear I miss you so. I love you so. I wish I were home. Writing to you helps.

God. Such an impressive array of thematic concerns, he thought to himself. This, he supposed, the general content of them all. This trip surely is widening her horizons. Bah. She'd practically brought the damn fellow along. In the back of her trip diary the days they would be gone were listed, and just before bed she would box the day's date off and then fill it in with pencil. One day less of captivity; the freedom to hug and kiss that moron one day closer.

He picked up her diary one day in Seville. She left the book out in the open, and since it was usually carefully hidden, he decided that she intended him to read it. He obliged: House of Duke of Alcala. Richest house in Southern Spain. They used marble dust, sand, and cactus juice to make the stucco. Jacqueline Kennedy had her debut in the courtyard. Tapestry. Armour. King Ferdinand's sword. Oh Bear. I wish you were here.

Cadiz: I miss Darren Bear so much. Today we saw orange trees. Sat in a park and Dad took my picture. I hope there are letters waiting for me at the American Express office. My aching heart. I wish my father understood what he means to me. Bear my love, my life. I miss your arms around me. Bah. Child. Father-thwarted, star-crossed lovers. Please, he sneered silently. Fifteen years old. Hardly the stuff of universal, divinely-sanctioned love. Fifteen. What was he doing at fifteen? Not this. Certainly not this.

No one had ever sent him letters day after day or written anything in diaries about him. No one said they couldn't live without his love; Mary in fact made it clear she would *rather* live without his love, didn't want it, spurned it, despised him.

He had a mental chart of the days his wife had been gone. Days had been huge at first, taking hours to cross off, but now they had shrunk to tiny bits you could drive a check mark through, and months were chunks the size of postage stamps. Moving farther and farther away from happiness, not towards it. His square pencil marks, those lead coffins he made pressing the pencil so hard it often broke, blended from a distance into a mass of dark grey past and future. Happiness is, he muttered. Happiness is . . . .

When she wasn't writing in her diary, or letters and postcards to him, or finding a post office, Rebecca was sleeping or staring hard and silent out the window. Out the window at the red poppies he too was looking at, the flocks of sheep with their shepherds, the tiny donkeys heavy laden by their masters. At the olive trees, the spindly telephone poles, the curvy winding road through the dry hills. And she, not he, getting car sick. That comes from trying to write in the car, he said. Tilt your head back; the fluid in your ears is what causes the problem. She threw up in a hotel lobby in Malaga. See? he said. See? I do know one thing or two, you know. I may be your father, but I'm also a doctor, and I'm not a *complete* idiot. Dad—she said. I'm going to my room to read.

Your evasion tactics aren't very subtle, you know, he said as she closed the door behind her. Hard to believe, but your old father has feelings too. Not that they matter.

Dad . . .

She who was Becky, age circa seven, helped him build his boat. He taught her to hold a screwdriver, then lifted her up on the deck to start screws for him. Then she wanted to make her own boat, only with the hammer. He showed her how to hold it lower down on the handle for a better swing. Then she took ends of wood from the scrap pile and hammered them together with spikes. Finishing nails made a railing around; rings of drywall nails made smokestacks. Tiny picture frame nails were people—many of them reclining. Dozens, even hundreds of nails. When the boat was finished, she took it down to the creek for the launch. He was invited along. Hammer scarred and nail laden, the boat tipped over and sank. I need to hammer on more wood, she said, fishing it out. For ballast.

Rebecca, you didn't finish your milk.
   So?

How strange to travel with someone you know so little, whose response to everything you say is either Dad, or Quit treating me like a child, or complete silence. She missed a lot, what with all the sleeping and letter writing. But she didn't want to hear about it. I'm going to lie down for a while, she'd say, and disappear for two or three hours.

   In Torremolinos she lay on the beach in a navy blue bikini, and he stood, startled, some twenty yards away. When did this woman begin to appear? This young woman was his daughter. His daughter this young woman. Not his child. Anymore. Not the same adolescent who wrote in the diary about her Bear and her breaking heart. This was the physical stuff of womanhood, and it threw him that he was so surprised. Fifteen. What does that mean? Oh Mary.

Rebecca, would you like a glass of wine with your dinner?
   Sure.

They were like different domestic animals sharing the same space. Quiet, mildly suspicious. Watchful. Dwight felt awkward now, uncomfortable and uncertain with her. He wished she would talk more; give him greater access to her thoughts, her self. This was a lonely way to travel.

In Granada he saw cigarettes in her suitcase. He should do

something, he decided. Be her father. So he threw them out, knowing even as he did so, and wincing, that there would be consequences.

Dad? I had some cigarettes in my suitcase and now they're gone. Did you take them?

Cigarettes! What are you doing with cigarettes?! You shouldn't have them anyway.

In other words you did.

That's not what I said. And don't speak to me that way.

—

Well yes I did. But you are not to smoke.

Oh.

Her anger and sullen silence lasted for two days. Until she found, he supposed, an international tobacconist's and bought some more. Fuck you, she seemed to be saying, leaving her purse ajar so he could see. I dare you. I dare you to do it again.

In Madrid, in the middle of the night, he woke up. Sat up. Looked to the dark curtains. No light came in. He could only assume he was there, in his pajamas, in the dark. Kids her age sleep a lot, he said to himself. It's normal. But next day he sent her back to the Prado for a set of postcards, and rifled through her luggage until he found the precious diary. Flicking through, his eyes caught common phrases and added them up. I am still jetlagged/ Tired today/ Slept 4 1/2 hours this afternoon/ Felt lousy this morning/ Felt nauseous on the bus/ Threw up that awful egg. It wasn't cooked long enough/ I'm very tired again today.

Oh Lord. Some doctor. He stared out the window at the cobbled, busy street in this foreign, foreign place, and cursed the boy. Cursed his wife. Cursed the world.

He stared hard out the window into the dark, his mind virtually paralyzed. He'd have to talk to her. Should talk to her. He should say—what? But she wouldn't talk. She'd go all cold and withdraw. What was the use? But he should talk to her, he insisted—must talk to her. How?

Silence.

His brother met them at the airport. The BMW was right outside the door; he would whisk them away home where Lenny waited, though Lenny had in fact acquired a nasty cut just yesterday morning. He'd been to the vet. Barbed wire, was the guess.

Uh, said Rebecca. I don't need a ride. Thanks but no thanks.

Standing over by a water fountain was the boy. Usually pale and freckled, he was lobster red with sunburn. Skin cancer candidate, that one. He wore a dark purple chiffon shirt that looked hideous against his skin. He wore dark sunglasses. And those pointy, scuffed black boots.

This boy had—this boy—Dwight's body trembled, with agitation, with loathing, with what might verge on despair. And then something in him gave and he just felt tired. Old. Stooped.

He watched his daughter rush into the arms of her beloved. He heard her say, Oh Bear. He stared at the boy's hands on her body, at his face nuzzled up to hers. What would happen now? Just what the hell would happen now?

DINOSAUR SUNDAY

My MOTHER, SHERRY said, grew up in Calgary. She told me that the gumbo mud was terrible in the spring, and stuck so thickly to the bottoms of their shoes they would have played men on the moon, only there weren't any yet.

I'd like to meet your Mum, Marc said.

Oh no you wouldn't, said Sherry.

Oh.

He wondered why, but didn't ask. He'd quickly learned she wouldn't answer him if she didn't want to anyway. And he didn't want to be ignored. What a girl. Her presence made him feel clumsy, cloddy. Even in his suit. Or maybe especially in his suit.

He had suggested the zoo. With great curiosity he had

watched the dinosaur park evolve on his way to work every day, had watched the mountains being constructed with wire, rocks, and what looked like plaster, watched the flat prairie zoo grounds transform into a prehistoric land. Now, for the first time, he was actually walking in it.

They did a pretty good job on this Dinosaur Park, didn't they, Sherry?

Looks kind of hokey to me. *You* don't think it's great, do you?

It's okay. But—

You know, she said, butting in, when I was seven we came to Calgary to visit my grandparents, she said, looking at him sideways and then taking his hand and swinging it. My sister and I climbed up on a dinosaur and had our picture taken. It wasn't one of these dinosaurs, though. The location doesn't feel right. Feels more like the dinosaur was over there somewhere.

I think it is over there. His name is Dinny. We can look, if you want.

I want. After. Relive the past and all that, you know. Seeing stuff you remember helps memory happen, I find. I haven't been to this zoo since then. Ever. We always went to Stanley Park, in Vancouver. They have flamingos there. And way more monkeys. They feed the wild animals chicken heads there, did you know? I saw a wheelbarrow full of chicken heads once. I stared and stared. Weirdest thing I ever saw.

Yuck.

Imagine the animals eating them. Crunch crunch crunch.

Like corn balls. Or pink and white jawbreakers.

Yuck.

It is yuck, isn't it? Let's change the subject. To something a little more serious. You'd like that, she said, nudging him.

On the telephone last night, he had accused her, ever so gently, of never taking him seriously, never talking about anything that really mattered, in the whole of the month or so they had been going out. At least, what mattered to him. Whenever he tried to bring up how he felt about her, eager, almost desperate, to get a sense of how she felt about him, she skittered off and talked about zany things. And now here she was, making fun of him.

Here's something interesting and serious at the same time, she said now. Have you ever thought how things used to be described in terms of nature, like, it looks like a big leaf, or it smells as nice as a forest, or it's as blue as the sky, and now it's backwards? Now the snow looks like styrofoam, that animal's coat is like velour. The clouds are like Dream Whip. Stuff like that. What does that *mean*, do you suppose?

I don't know. Never thought about it much.

Neither do I. Know what? You have nice blond hair on your hands. And on your arms. Undo your cuff so I can see, okay? You're all tied up so tight, like a package or something. A fancy package, however. Aren't you hot in that suit?

He wished he were wearing a t-shirt; his muscles were, he believed, his most redeeming feature. He pumped iron four nights a week, and he thought she might like him better if she could see the results more clearly. But she had wanted the suit. Said she liked how young men looked coming out of church. Brother. What kind of a chump was he, to succumb to this?

Where did your family live in Calgary, Sherry? Ouch! Sorry. Couldn't resist. First down by the river on 38th Street. That's where the gumbo mud was. Then in Mount Royal, once my grandfather got more successful.

Why shouldn't I want to meet your mother? If you don't mind my asking.

I don't much feel like talking about it, actually, Sherry said, her voice suddenly cool, light, distant. It's too nice a day. In my opinion.

There was a pause. Then Marc said, low, grumbling, I don't know why I wore this dumb thing anyway.

You mean your monkey suit? Sherry said, nudging him again.

Most appropriate, don't you think? Let's go see your pals now, okay? She laughed and slipped her arm around his waist, put her hand in his left pocket.

He had met her at the C-train station. She was pacing up and down the platform and reading at the same time, and she'd walked right into him. Sorry, she said, and started talking. She liked to read while she waited for the train, she said, because she thought it was like being in a movie. She'd been hoping to meet someone in just this way, actually, had been trying for several weeks now to casually bump into someone, but people tended to step out of the way. Now it had finally happened. Fate. Had he read this collection of short stories by Cecelia Frey? He should. It was excellent. And she's a Calgary writer, too, she added significantly. Then she told him that she'd just been volunteering at the Kerby Centre. Wednesday was dancing day. Every Wednesday afternoon she wheeled her Betty down to watch Reg and the others foxtrot and two-step. To a real band. Going to Twinkle Toes, they called it. Here she did a couple of steps and a twirl, to illustrate. Did he dance? Her name was Sherry. And she went to university; Drama; spring session had just started. What did he do?

His mind churned and thudded. He couldn't think of a thing to say in the face of such energy. She was a humming-bird and he was a slug. He was instantly crazy about her. Work, he said, wishing he were an entrepreneur, or an inventor, something even faintly exotic. I'm going home from work. Insurance. Boring. I went to U. of C. too, he added hopefully. B.Sc., 1989.

You remind me of my mother when you say that, Sherry said.
  Say what? Marc asked, startled.
  Dee dee dee dee, under your breath like that.
  Oh did I? Sorry.
  That's okay. I don't always hate her.
  —
Would you like an ice cream cone, Sherry?
  Sure.
  Sitting on a picnic table, periodically licking up and

around the sides of their cones, Sherry and Marc sat side by side in silence. He loosened his tie, undid the top two buttons on his shirt.

You have blond hair there, too, she said. Ooh.

What's that supposed to mean? he said, blushing slightly.

Why don't you take off your jacket?

Sure. Hold my cone?

Sure.

They smiled at each other. They finished their ice cream. He enclosed one of her hands in his. Now we're getting somewhere, he thought. But then she heaved a big sigh of what seemed to be resolve. She stood up and sat down. It was like she had wings and was about to take off and then decided against it. He wished she would sit still for five minutes.

Can I tell you something? she said.

Yes. Just don't fly away on me.

I really need to tell someone because I don't understand. I just don't understand how anyone could be so mean. It hurts just to think about it.

Who's mean? he said.

My mother. My mummy. You mustn't interrupt, all right? You mustn't say a word until I'm finished or I'll cry, and then I'll never forgive you.

Okay.

She took a deep breath and the words tumbled out.

My mother lives in Calgary. I wanted you to think I was here all by myself, because that's more interesting. She lives on Pump Hill. Three Saturdays ago I thought I'd just drop in to see her. Usually I phone first. But that day I thought I'd be spontaneous. I hadn't seen her in ages. There were all these tables on the front lawn. Like at a community hall dance. She must have rented them. There wasn't much stuff left. Hey you didn't tell me you were having a garage sale, Mum! I says. Why didn't you call me? I could have helped. She looks kind of around and down and puts on her I'm a doddery old lady who is verging on senile except I'm still a little young for it routine and says Oh didn't I? I thought I did. Didn't I call you on Wednesday? It must have slipped my mind. And then this guy comes waltzing out of the house carrying the brass pole lamp from the living room. He says can he come back for it later because it won't fit in his car. That'll be fine, my mother says. When he's gone I say Why'd you sell that? That's a nice lamp! It's always been in the living room. Between the nesting tables and the sideboard. That's where it belongs. Well, she says, kind of funny. The nesting tables. . . . And then I knew. Terror gripped my heart, I tell you, Marc, as I raced into the house. The living room was practically empty. There was just the entertainment centre left. And an African mask on one wall and a Guatemalan weaving on another. That's it. Mum!! I scream—I literally screamed, Marc— where *is* everything?! Where did everything *go*?

I'm not *precisely*, not completely, sure of the answer to that, says my mother. Would you like a glass of lemonade?

No. No I wouldn't. I was really mad by then. What I want is to know why you've sold darn near everything in the house. Are you broke or something?

It's rude to pry, says my mother.

It's rude to sell my history without telling me, I retort.

Well if you insist. No, I am not financially strained, she says. I just wanted a change.

A change. She sold off everything, Marc. Everything except stuff she gathered on her own trips. Woven hangings from Brazil. Male and female tea cups from Japan, silver jewellery from Mexico. I don't care about that stuff, Marc. That's just *her* stuff. I don't care! There's nothing left from Gramma and Grampop's house. Gone. Nesting tables, lamps, sideboard, dining room table. All the china and my favourite hassock and even the lacy pillowslips and eiderdown quilts. My past is gone, don't you see? I'll float away! Why'd she do it? Why'd she do it, Marc?

He tried to look concerned. He pushed his palms against each other and flexed his pecs. He opened his mouth.

Well I know, she said, her voice angry and wavery with tears. I asked her. Do you know what she said? You want to know what she said? She said she felt fettered by the past.

Huh?

Fettered. To the past. Gosh she gets so melodramatic sometimes. She said she felt she was being dragged backwards, wasn't free to be herself, she said. Felt the rocks of ages tied to her feet. Picture that, Marc.

That's too bad, said Marc.

For who? she demanded.

For you. I guess.

Too bad. Too, too, bad. It sure as heck is. It's not just the stuff, you see. I'm not saying where's my inheritance. It's that I feel as though there's nothing behind me but big empty space. Like blank landscape. Like this before they stuck the dinosaurs in. Like I come from nowhere except her and now she wants to be unfettered so where does that leave me? Oh now I'm barren, she said dramatically, wrist to forehead, eyes closed. I'm historically barren.

Did you—

You know what she said? Do you want to know what she said, Marc? She said, and I quote, Oh those old things. Oh those old things. Can you believe it? She gave me three pictures. The frames were broken so nobody wanted to buy them. Pictures of my relatives. Except my mother can't remember who they are, and it doesn't say on the back. Whoever they are, they're on my wall now. Above my bed. They're all I've got.

He reached out to put his arm around her. You've got me, if that's anything.

Silence ensued. This unnerved him, but he spoke again. Maybe she wasn't thinking about you, he said slowly. Maybe she was just thinking about what she needed to do.

But what about me?

Well, poor Sherry. I guess.

Don't poor Sherry me, she said, sitting up straight, and hard.

After an uncomfortable pause he asked, So what was it like when your Mum moved to Pump Hill?

She's been there forever.

Not forever. It hasn't been there forever.

The hill has. Not the people. Well, years and years. There was no landscaping or anything when she moved in. Just mud and new houses. No grass, no trees, nothing. Like this here, only way muddier and uglier.

Did you feel awful like this when she first moved there?

Gosh, I don't remember. Maybe I did.

You got over it, though.

Must have. I don't remember.

Then you'll get over this, too.

I don't want to get over this, Marc, she said coldly, pulling away and looking him in the eye. It matters too much. God. You sound like her or something.

Eventually you will. I'll bet.

It sounds very much as though you assume you'll be around to see that day.

Hey, I'm not assuming anything, Sherry. But you'll have to get over it. You can't expect people to go around not changing just because it doesn't suit you.

Thanks for the support, she said, rising. I ought to get going now.

Hey, don't get all mad. You wouldn't not change for someone. Not for a second. Would you?

Maybe.

Please sit down again? Please?

She sat down.

He counted to twenty and began. You know, as I was trying to say earlier, this isn't like it was when the dinosaurs were here, either. They couldn't survive in this park.

I know that. This is fake.

No no. I mean in Drumheller like it is now, either. There's nothing for them to eat. There used to be grass, and water, and weeds and stuff for them to eat. Not much but a few rattlers, and maybe some antelope, survive in this kind of landscape.

Couldn't they adapt?

To what? To no water? No food?

I guess not.

Adapt or die, and they couldn't, so they did.

Huh.

She swayed a bit and then leaned against his chest. Her face was warm against his shirt and his skin. She said, You know, I'm lucky to have you. You're brilliant.

No I'm not, he said, and put his arm around her. Then, very carefully, he lowered his cheek to the top of her head. He loved the smell of her hair, loved the pulse in her taut, small body.

Hey Marc?

Yes.

I can be a real pain, can't I?

Yes.

Hey. Look at *those* dinosaurs. They've really had to adapt.

Two small children walked by, waving their inflatable dinosaurs up and down, up and down, on the sticks to which they were tethered.

FINDING
LINETTE

CHRISTMAS CAKE AND rum and Coke. My mother and her husband greet us in their matching slippers and plaid flannel dressing gowns. They have set out plates and glasses and ice on the kitchen counter. I have something for Bowser, too, says my mother, and he hears his name and starts to shiver with anticipated pleasure. My mother bends carefully over and opens a cupboard. Takes out a can. Sticks a green prefab bow on top. Hands it to me. You can open this and give it to him if you like. Every year, my father bought each dog a can of salmon. Do you remember that? And so this is for Bowser. Good dog. Bowser gobbles up the salmon in under ten seconds. Then burps. Wags heartily. This is a good place.

On Christmas Eve, I set my laptop on a Pakistani hassock. Mum? Will you tell me about Linette now?

I suppose.

Can we start with her mother?

Yes.

The very beginning I know. I write:

One day in 1948, a young woman from California came to Banff on the train. She saw my father at the Banff Clinic, became his patient.

Later, more lines on the computer: *Linette's mother, Stelloise, was average. Average height, weight, intelligence. Midbrown hair.*

That's all?

Well—my mother says, after a long pause, after reading disappointment on my face—it was reddish brown, though not auburn. And—she didn't wear her hair loose. She wore it tied up, in a bun. That could be significant.

My mother looks tired, distracted. She leans back, closes her eyes, goes limp, as though she's been the vehicle for a voice from the other side, and the visitation has ended.

My husband and Oscar are sitting side by side on the chesterfield, reading magazines—*Outside,* my husband, *Time,* Oscar—and drinking rum and Coke. They aren't really here. Neither is Bowser. He is whimpering in puppy dreams. His muzzle and whiskers are soiled with a paste of chewed rawhide bone and saliva. My husband gets up, goes over to him, strokes him. It's okay. Good dog. Good dog.

Her father was supposed to be an Italian. She had slightly olive

124

skin, and dark eyes and hair. Italian features. She was slightly
blue at birth, too.

Remember the Delmonico baby? The only daughter? She
was blue at birth too. Remember that?

She's come up behind me, startled me. I've been staring at
my reflection in the dark window, thinking how it's like a
darker me is caught in the pane.

Yes. I'm working on the father part right now. Tell me
more about the father, will you?

Nobody knew anything.

Not even Stelloise?

Let's see.

There were two versions of what happened. The first was that
she had been raped by this man. But after a while, a different
story came out.

(Came out? Came out of where? Stelloise's mouth? Thin
air? A deceptively empty shell at the beach?)

That story was that she had had a love affair with this man,
this Italian, but he left her.

(Left? Dumped? Moved away? Love affair. Not just affair;
love affair.)

I've got to sit down. My knee is bothering me. Oscar?
Would you make me another drink? That last one was
excellent.

My mother's bed in the hospital was beside hers. They talked, my
mother tells me, but not very much. About babies, mostly; about

my mother's new baby Laurel, and the six-year-old Marnie at home; about Linette. When Linette's mother went back to California, back to palm trees and orange trees and ocean, she left Linette with my mother.

No no no. That isn't right.

She's back.

What isn't?

Your *cousin* was born a week apart from Linette. That was in August. Laurel wasn't born until the following February.

Marnie still plays on the floor. My aunt stands to one side with my cousin. Laurel vanishes. My mother is pregnant, with one baby on her knee.

Then how *did* you meet Stelloise?

I met her at the hospital.

Did you visit her?

No! My mother is exasperated. She goes back to her chair, picks up her knitting. I went there to pick up the *baby!* she says, and lays into a row.

Okay okay.

At Dad's, the four sisters will converge. We will be together for the first time in more than five years. Weather permitting. There is a huge amount of snow this year. Trouble, personal despair, permitting. There is some of that around. I'll ask them all about Linette, Stelloise. Anything they can remember, or remember having heard.

At Dad's the Christmas tree has just tipped over, and Marnie and her son, Will, and Dad are trying to put it right.

We'll be with you in a minute, says Marnie. Come on in, says my father. We're glad to see you, even if we look a little preoccupied. There. That ought to do.

Into the kitchen. A small libation, anyone?

Marnie says Look, Bowser, and reaches to the top of the fridge. This is for you. Maybe you don't remember, Ann, but every year, Grandpop bought each of the dogs a can of tuna. Here is your tuna, Bowser. This is for you. Biff has already had his, so keep him away.

Biff is round and spotted. He looks like the dog in the Pavlov cartoon. Bowser tolerates him, but wishes he were more of a one for playing. Biff's a little too formal for that. He's a spectator dog.

Bowser wolfs down the tuna in under ten seconds. Burps. Wags happily. Asks to go outside. Throws up on the porch.

Cookie decorations litter the counter—candy sprinkles, tiny silver balls, Smarties.

Where are all the cookies? I ask. Where are the cookies you made? I can't smell baking.

The baking soda didn't work, says Marnie glumly. It was probably ten years old. And only the top burner in the oven works.

We mock accusing looks at Dad. He looks innocent.

Before we see Laurel, we see her four children struggling up the driveway with their sleeping bags and pillows. Then we see our sister, loaded down with bags and suitcases and a half gallon of white wine. They have come from the ferry; they have come from Campbell River. We run out into the snow. Let me carry something. Here, I'll carry that. She puts everything down, and we hug. Hard. Laurel cries. She always does.

Roberta and her two little boys arrive after supper. It was an icy, snowy, scary trip down from the Cariboo, and she is exhausted. Her son Geoffrey, determined not to fall asleep before he got to his grandfather's house, bored her silly playing Guess What I'm Thinking Now, and Name That Tune that he tapped out on the seat with his five year old fingers. She grabs an ashtray and someone pours her a glass of wine.

Now we are four. We've done it. Nothing, finally, has thwarted us. Quick, I say. Take a picture. No! We look terrible. We look tired and washed out. So what? I say. If one of us drops dead in the night, we'll have no record. So in a weary row we put our arms around each other and smile.

I lie in the van against my sleeping husband's back and feel very very happy. I don't know when I've been so happy and so tired at the same time.

My sister Marnie carefully pushed my carriage back and forth when I was a baby. She told me stories she made up about Little Green and Little Purple Riding Hoods. Variations on

The Three Bears. She taught Roberta to read by making a little book about Hitler. Hitler is good. I like Hitler. Hitler has candy for Roberta. She taught us camp songs from the Sierra Nevada. When she came back from Thailand, she taught me words and said I was quick to learn. She sent me a piece of red Singapore silk.

My sister Laurel told me fairy stories she learned from the fairies she knew. She and Roberta locked themselves in the bedroom closet and went to fairyland. I wasn't allowed. They came out with beatific expressions on their faces, and Laurel would tell me about the wondrous things they had seen, about the fabric of the fairies' dresses, about the kind and loving things the fairies had said to them. I was dying to go. No. You are too little.

My sister Laurel and I spent a lot of time down at the creek. We shinnied up trees and named havens; we played Tarzana and Tarzeena. Roberta didn't come. She had asthma. Allergic to everything, cats, feathers, pollen, horses, house dust. Our bedroom at night so often filled with steam from kettles.

My sister Roberta fell out of one of the big cedars onto her head. She was knocked out. Laurel and I laughed because we didn't know what to do. Roberta was playing fairies by herself on the day new tile was put in her bedroom. There were bricks stacked on her bed. She floated backwards off the bed stead and bashed her head.

In addition to the Ghostbuster car that is the hit of the holidays among the children, and Mutant Turtle slippers with eyes that Bowser will chew off, Roberta has brought three big tins of peanut butter cookies, Nanaimo bars, fudge-filled meringues. Bags of Christmas candies, ribbon, red white and green gum drops, and nougat, which I've always hated because she liked it. (It's the same with doughnuts. And White Spot restaurants.) Christmas, she says, is very important to her. She is the most extravagant of us all at Christmas; she loads on the gifts. She is, too, the conciliatory one. In all seasons.

Through the morning we drink pots of coffee. Reach for cookies and candies. Chase children and dogs outside.

You guys, I say, I want to find the things about Linette. Desperately. Does anyone know where they are?

I think I have the baby book somewhere, says Laurel. But maybe not. I seem to remember Mum saying I couldn't have it for some reason. I remember seeing the letters here. And maybe her birth certificate.

I think I remember seeing some of that here, says Marnie.

On the little blue bookshelf, says Laurel.

Yes. In a thick file folder with some letters. But it isn't there anymore. Dad, do you have any idea?

No idea. I haven't touched a thing down there.

I know. We can tell.

We all laugh.

Downstairs, where a rec room would be if there were one, across from the fireplace with its metal tabs sticking through the concrete, are wide wooden shelves. On these shelves are tins of soup, of crab, of salmon, of white asparagus and hearts of palm. There are gift baskets sent in years past, too special to open. At one end, but amongst this still, fishing gear. Boxes and boxes of flies. Fishing maps, charts, nets, rolls of fly line. Behind and beside these are boxes of old photographs. McGill yearbooks. Plastic Christmas decorations too tacky to use. Broken lamps, a wok set, suitcases. A pair of silver hair brushes that belonged to my mother's father.

The box I pull down from the top shelf is a tumble of time. Dad at Lingnan University and me at thirteen with my ballet trophy. Marnie as a wee girl in Banff feeding a fawn, my mother's parents shortly after their wedding, he with spats, she with long white gloves. Colour photos, daguerreotypes, black and white, flat and glossy. Faces and events gone long enough to surprise us with their reappearance.

We all have become bigger, I notice. And as I look through the photograph albums, I see that it is no wonder. Our ancestors were sturdy women. Some small before, until marriage, but all big later on. We are getting later on.

I climb back up the shelves and pull down more stuff. Fat file folders of pictures each of us drew at art lessons; wax crayons, tempera, water colours. Rich blues and greens.

Roberta drew lovely controlled hyacinths, two-tone purple.

Roberta drew fine red tulips with elegant long green leaves, and bright yellow daffodils with golden yellow centres.

I drew dogs.

Laurel bounces down the stairs. I'm a Tigger, I'm a Tigger, I'm Tigger the only one. Look at all these dog pictures. You must have drawn these, Ann.

I did. I like dogs.

No kidding. You were always getting bitten by dogs. Remember? You'd run up to strays and throw your arms around them. And then they'd bite you.

You got bitten on the face once, says Roberta.

So that's what happened. Laurel fakes stifling a laugh, and ducks.

Ha ha, I say.

Remember Jerry?

Sort of. He was black, with a white tip on his tail.

Remember he bit you?

No he didn't. I liked Jerry and he liked me.

Yes he did. You tried to make him eat mud pies. You grabbed him by the head and tried to shove his nose into these little mounds of mud. Come *on*, Jerry, you said. So he bit you.

Poor me.

Poor Jerry, you mean.

He got hit by a car and we didn't find him for several days, until the store people phoned and said he was there, says Roberta. We went with Dad to get him, and Dad made Laurel carry a corner of the sack he'd brought to carry him on. We thought he was so mean for making you do that. You were crying so hard. We buried him down by the creek. Somebody made him a cross with his name on it in blue tacks.

That was me, says Laurel. Dad helped me.

You guys, I really want to find the Linette stuff.

Okay. Okay, we'll help look. We're sorry. They look lovingly at me. I am the little sister again. I am loved.

I *feel* that the stuff is here, says Laurel.

Great. Do you *feel* where?

Why did Mum want to take another child? I ask Marnie. She has cobwebs in her hair. Our hands are brown with dust, our clothes are smeared with dust. You were six, and she was pregnant with Laurel . . .

She always wanted to have two children close in age, so they could be friends. Like you and Roberta. She looks at me with a look. This was her big chance.

Oh, I say.

I kiss my sisters often; I hug them often. I cannot express in words what I want to convey. Touching, holding. I can call I love you into a void, I can say I love you to a gravestone, I can write I love you in a letter, or say it over the phone. But, I think to them, I cannot hold you, and feel our breasts squash against each other and maybe hear your heart or your breath, and smell your hair and feel the warmth of you.

The four of us sit in the living room. The inevitable Joan Sutherland sings in slightly more than the background.

Quick, somebody, turn her off.

He'll be back in a minute and turn her back on anyway.

I'm really annoyed, you know? Where the hell is all this stuff? It belongs to all of us, not one of us or none of us.

Well—

Well—

Well—

Shut up, you guys. I'll just write what I know, to start with. I write: *Linette was sick; she had pneumonia; she had to go to the hospital in Calgary. My mother left Laurel and Marnie with a neighbour, wrapped Linette in a yellow blanket, and boarded the train.*

She sat down by a window that let her see backwards. She looked out at elk grazing by the railway crossing.

Ann? says Marnie, reading over my shoulder. We were living in Field. The train was going from Field to Banff. That's where the hospital was, not Calgary. And I don't know how the elk were grazing. It was March; there was still a lot of snow.

Okay. Why were you living in Field? This is all news to me. It isn't a matter of not remembering, it's one of never knowing.

Dad could make more money there or something, I think, says Laurel.

Money? says our father. That's not it! His cheeks are pink from standing out on the porch filling the bird feeders, and he stamps his feet a little as he speaks. He takes off his gloves and puts them on top of the book case, makes a place for them amongst a variety of different candles in various stages of life and death.

Money. That's not it at all. We were in Field because the doctor there had a heart attack. My father was a doctor for the CPR, and he was responsible for making sure a replacement doctor was sent. He sent me. We were there for eight or nine months. Your mother hated it, as I recall. A railroad town.

Did the other doctor die?

No. He got better and we moved back to Banff.

My mother wrapped the baby Linette in a yellow blanket, left the other two children with a neighbour, and boarded the train for Banff.

She sat down by a window that let her see backwards. She looked out at elk grazing through the snow by the railway crossing.

That's not quite right either, says Laurel, looking over my shoulder.

Yes, says my father, reading too, his arm around Laurel.

Laurel says, Linette and I were in bassinets on the train, side by side.

But *that* isn't true, says Marnie. You weren't there.

Where was I then? There is a note of defiance in her voice.

With a neighbour, probably.

But I've always been there. I've always been told that.

Well . . .

How can you remember anyway? I ask suddenly. You were a tiny baby; you were younger than Linette.

It doesn't really matter, does it, you guys? says Roberta.

I don't know how I know. I've just always known. It's just part of me. There was a pink bank and a blue bank, too. I don't know what happened to them. I wanted hers so badly, though, and she wasn't around any more. So one day I climbed up on the window sill and got it and smashed it. There were pink and blue hairbrushes, too, I think.

I remember propping her up and helping her drink her bottle, Marnie says. She got out of breath so easily.

She had a hole in her heart, right?

Yes. A defective heart muscle, says Dad. She didn't thrive. That's what we say about such babies. We were going to send her to have an operation in Toronto. Everything was set up. But she had to be a certain size, a certain weight before they could safely operate.

And then she caught pneumonia.

That's right.

I write: *The baby Linette is pale beside her robust sister. Apple blossom and apple. White, red. There are worlds between them in health. One baby hollers heartily and flails sturdy limbs happily and angrily about. The other baby lies virtually noiseless beside her. She has a hole in her heart.*

She was never pale, says Marnie. Her skin was dark from not having enough oxygen in her blood.

I think it was just the three of us on the train, by the way. Dad's voice comes over from the La-Z-Boy where he sits with his *New York Times* crossword. The four of us and our mother bought that chair for him. It is getting worn out now; the brown is out of the vinyl in high touch areas, where his head rests, his shoulders. He looks at us over his Mulroney glasses. I think it was just the three of us, he repeats. Your mother and I, and the child.

The four of us exchange glances. We've never heard *this* before. With it we are reminded that our mother deletes him from everything, has taken scissors and cut him out, sometimes carefully, sometimes carelessly. But he was there. He went on the train.

Where was I then?

With a neighbour, probably, with me, Marnie says. They wouldn't have a healthy baby like you along. It'd be too much work.

And Ann?

Yes Dad?

We rode in the caboose.

The caboose?!

Yes. It was winter. March, I think. There were many more freight trains going through in those days than passenger trains. We rode in the caboose to Banff. There was a lot of snow that year.

I rode in the caboose too, says Marnie. Before she did, though. I rode in the caboose when I had appendicitis. But it wasn't fair, because I was in too much pain to enjoy it.

She died on the train.

Yes. We hadn't even left the station.

Why didn't you get off?

I suppose we didn't know what to do, so we just kept going.

As the train pulled out of the station, she drew the blanket back to see the sweet face. Linette was dead.

She rode all the way, all the way to Calgary with the dead baby in her arms. Oh God, I said. How sad for you! And what if someone asked to see her? See the dear baby's precious face? What if someone wanted to stroke her cheek or feel her tiny fingers curl around a finger? Oh how that must have felt to hold her, so still, while the train jolted beneath you. How did it feel in your heart? The tiny body so newly alive and so newly dead, still warm, still bundled pink and white.

No one asked to see her, said my mother.

I very much want to save this part, want it to be part of the truth. But now it can't. It will have to go.

Mum came back without Linette, says Marnie. Linette was just gone. I remember crying and crying. Later, I wanted to know why Linette couldn't have a lamb gravestone like Helen had. Why can't Linette have a lamb? I asked. Why can't she have a lamb like Helen's lamb? People said she wasn't really your sister. But that wasn't right. She was my sister.

We are quiet for quite a long time. Then Laurel says, Her

mother named her Linette. Mum added the Ruth.

Dad? I ask. What was Stelloise like?

Oh she was a nice enough girl. Blonde, I think. But not a frizzy blonde.

This is all so depressing, says Roberta. Let's sing or something.

That woman sounds as though she's in pain, says Laurel, rolling her eyes at the stereo, and we laugh and look at Dad, who raises his eyebrows. Hmm? he says. Who's in pain?

Could we turn her off, do you think?

I don't see why not. Don't tell me though—please don't tell me—that none of my four girls have learned to appreciate a fine singing voice?

Dad—

Dad—

Dad—

Dad—

Wait'll you hear us.

Roberta plays the piano and we sing Christmas carols and songs from the *Fireside Book of Folk Songs*. Ann used to wander around the house with this book, Marnie says. Singing away. *Barbara Allen*, they say in unison and laugh. We sing 'The Skye Boat Song,' 'Muss I Den,' 'Bendemeer's Stream,' 'Loch Lomond.' 'The Blue Bells of Scotland.' 'Peter Gray,' scalpi-ed by a bloody Indian and his girl Lucy, who wept and wept and wep-i-ed her poor sweet life away. Exuberance and laughter. 'Joe Hill,' 'Raggle Taggle Gypsies,' 'Careless Love.'

In the morning I come carefully in from the van. Behind the front door are small sleeping bodies, my nephews and niece. They will remember this when they grow up, I think. Remember camping in the foyer when they came to visit their grandfather.

It is still dark outside. I am the first in the kitchen, then Laurel, then Marnie, then Roberta. Beth comes in and hugs quietly against Laurel. What will she remember about us?

We have talked about many things in the past two days. I have, through the others, recovered parts of myself I'd forgotten. Fragments of history, pieces of our family. Maybe my sisters have too. I am much calmer, I think, happier deep inside, when we hug goodbye.

We have talked, too, about our plagues of individual unhappiness. They have come, will come, at different times. Mine is over, for the time being, anyway. I've stopped drinking, smoking. I seem truly happy, say my sisters, and they are right. Marnie's is too, I think, or at least she is irrevocably on the way. Laurel's is in full black and red blossom, and Roberta's is still gestating, bubbling, building inside. We help each other. We do not, the four of us, lack inner fortitude.

How glad I am that none of us is an only child, says Laurel, in tears again. Think how it would be not to have each other like this.

As my husband and I drive home to Calgary along the icy

highway, up along the Coquihalla deeply banked in snow, I think about Linette. I think how her unmarked grave has always appealed to, has heightened, our sense of kinship, of family and its secrets, of Romance. There is something delicious—but that can't be the right word—about knowing something that no one else knows, and we know about that grave.

I asked my father why they didn't get her a gravestone. I guess I don't remember, he said. I'm not sure. Well she wasn't really one of the family, you see. Dear, I don't know. I was busy in those days.

But you buried her in the family plot . . .

I don't know, dear. And he became uneasy and edgy. Maybe he doesn't want to remember, maybe all this prying into the past is pain.

The four of us stand, an elderly semi-circle, around the pink granite marker. Two of us wear hats, with flowers. Laurel lays baby's breath on the grave. We smile sadly at each other.

From time to time for the rest of our lives, I suppose, the four of us will talk about getting a gravestone for Linette. One year I got as far as pricing pink granite. But nothing happened. I suppose we feel she has gotten this far without a gravestone, and money for such a romantic notion is harder to come by than money for the dentist or *The Phantom of the Opera*. Romance seldom suits the present. It is the stuff of longing for other than the now, for the future, for the past, for another set of circumstances.

How odd a brand new stone would look forty years later anyway. And what would you put on such a stone?

Linette. Maybe that would be enough.

LOVED DAUGHTER

Every year, you took your four daughters to Banff, and every year we competed to see who would remember the names of the mountains, of Brewster, Sulphur, Goat, and Cascade; of Rundle, Tunnel, Stony Squaw. And every time, we argued over who got to be the Three Sisters. Banff was ours, somehow, because you grew up there. It was the others, the tourists, who didn't belong.

Whenever I go to Banff now, on my own, I still do the ritual tour. I go to see the merman; I go past the two houses you lived in—Spray Avenue, and Buffalo Street; I go past the United church; I go to the graveyard. I like to stand at these places and think how you and your family filled this exact same space I'm filling, only a long time ago. How you looked at the same mountain I am looking at now. That you and your family climbed these very steps. That maybe you stood on the bank of the Bow exactly where I'm standing now. That you walked through the door of the Paris café, maybe, as I've just done, and past the Lux theatre, taking these very same steps.

Until yesterday, I left out going to the dump to see the bears. It's not the sort of thing you do alone. But on a whim I thought I'd go again. It was quite the surprise to find the dump moved, and to learn that you can't watch the bears anymore anyway.

After the dump, or rather, after going to the space that used to be filled with the dump, and the bears, I went to the graveyard. Drove up past your big white house on the river. You said it was surrounded by deep forest when you moved in, that the pine needles were thick on the ground. Not anymore. I parked outside the gate of the graveyard, and walked across diagonally, pausing at the Brett mausoleum. From there I looked for the lamb. As I always do.

I can stand and look at that lamb for a long, long time.

She was only five years old. Barely five years old in 1933. You, the eldest, were sixteen.

You, in your mid-seventies now. Still finding it difficult to talk about her; still shying away.

You've told me that your mother borrowed kettles from all the neighbours. You will never forget the smell, you said, of the tincture of benzoin and menthol.

146

Borrowed kettles boiling turbulent and hot in the kitchen, brought with pot holders and oven mitts steaming up the stairs, up carpeted stairs, into your sister's sick room.

You couldn't see in for the steam. Out your own bedroom door you saw the warm fog tumble out into the hall, felt the moisture like wet moss on the carpet runner in the hall, saw the wallpaper peeling off around the door frames. The carpets were damp for days, you said. You remember the quieting hush-hushes blending the quiet steps, the go-on-to-bed-now-dear. You remember your sister's small tired coughs, the rasping rattle in her chest as she tried to breathe.

You remember hearing the other doctor come to your house. Your father's competition, rival, the doctor who had never set foot in your house before, the man you had never seen close up before. That's when you realized how sick she was.

Heard that other doctor's footsteps on the wet walk, the weight on the front steps and veranda. You peeked out your window, wiped the steam off first with your hand and then with your pajama top, and saw that other doctor reach for the heavy door knocker and then change his mind and lower his hand and rap lightly instead, then with both hands touch the door and ease it open and enter the dim light of the foyer. The brown doctor bag identical to your father's. The woollen scarf. The black great coat. You-the-boy shivered by the window in your bare feet and feared the situation so dire that your father, your, to you, omnipotent father, could not handle alone.

You moved away from the window and closer to your bedroom door and heard the two men come heavily up the stairs, heard the two doctor voices, the low and solemn bass lines, pass your door. The brief light voice of your mother down the hall, shards of light sad sound. Then her going down the stairs to put more water on.

The windows were wet inside and outside.

What did the other children hear and see? They must have felt, along with their oldest brother, some of the heaviness of heart; they must have felt the bone-chilling fog of grief descending, enshrouding their house.

Just past her fifth birthday. Was there a party? Cakes and candles and presents for the youngest darling? Candy baskets. Party favours. A peanut hunt. Nickels in the cake.

The internment was at your house. She lay in a small white coffin in front of the grand piano. Grampie slept beside her Saturday and Sunday nights so she wouldn't be alone.

There was a graveside service on Monday. On Monday, you went with her, drew a mourning line from home to grave. Up Buffalo Street where you sledded, where she caught her cold.

There is the lamb. On the tombstone the tiny white lamb all mossy around the ears now, all dirty around the mouth.

I stand in front of the family plot, and imagine that I am standing exactly where you stood. I see breath in the early winter air. Hot tears steam and turn cold on your cheeks. Here. Right here with me.

HIDING
AMONG
THE TREES

Back over the rockies.
Dragged unwilling back home on a line and tackle. Reeled
in across boulders, crevasses, bumping and falling; cutting
and bruising.

Clean jeans and t-shirt, her father's olive pullover. Hardly
bereavement attire. No B on her forehead. No outer sign that
her mother is dead.

Hair of the dog. Scale of the fish.

Out the window, through patches of cloud, she sees the
careful squares of yellow and brown land. A milky sheen of frost
covers the surface, a faint mist grows as the mountains approach.

She drinks straight from the miniature. Succour.

Only one hour this way. From here to there. Which is
which when a person is suspended above the mountains?

Pressure builds in the descent to Vancouver. The wheels touch ground and the plane yanks back against wet tarmac. It is pouring rain, pounding, drowning rain, belting out of the sky, belting onto the black tarmac, onto the dense green trees. Let me out of here. Let that rain drench me.

Years ago, her mother flooded the living room with cut glass. She lined it up on all the ledges. Put prisms in all the windows, strung all the way across on fishing line. Dabs of light all over everything. Three big crystal bowls on the coffee table. Candy dishes, relish dishes, a mustard server. Glasses from sherry to champagne. Jam jars on the sideboard. Decanters, boxes, butter dishes. Crystal on every surface in the room. Empty.

Her mother pauses at the tall windows and runs her hands across the prisms, sets them all to swinging, and she turns round and round, smiling, her long diamond earrings swinging, the diamond bracelet on her left wrist glittering. Light bounces madly, rainbow colours and piercing glances from the diamonds skitter all over her and the room.

Come and dance with me, Peggy! Come and catch the rainbows! See them all over my arms? Are they all over my face too? Come and dance with me, Peg.

No. It's stupid.

Dear one, you're so solemn these days. Catch some of this light.

No.

Last night, another bender. Back into the liquor with her full attention. Bend me out of shape. Each bottle a thin layer of shellac, of strengthener. Drop me on my head, and only the insides shatter.

I was only going to drink three drinks. Again. Guzzle guts. Drink until it's done.

Avoid the undesirables, Peggy. I know, I know, mother. As you screw on a diamond earring, as you examine yourself in the mirror to make sure your ears match. You've got it wrong. *I* am undesirable, mother. You should have seen me last night. No one would have wanted me.

That last dirty mother a stiff one. An inch of milk. An ounce of Kahlua, an ounce of tequila. Approximately. A good swift shot into sleep. Tobacco, sour milk, and liqueur-coated mouth this morning.

Back into it for sure. Back into it to the teeth, to the eyes. Drink me.

Ashtrays jammed with butts. Cluster of bottles by the back door. Kicked them over. Stood them up. The whole place a disaster area this morning. The last crystal wine glass, coated in milk, broken, by her foot.

Good thing I live alone.

MacTac on the cardboard closet doors. Phentex owl on the living room wall. Pink arborite counters all scarred from knife cuts. What a place. Home? Never home.

Out the apartment window strobe light glimpses of the river, snippets of dark water. The current growing stronger and colder every day. The cold artery of dark water moving smoothly towards the city.

Last night Monica tapped lightly and stood china-faced on
her door sill. No costume. No make-up.
    Can I talk to you, Peg?
    Go to hell, Monica.
    Listen just for a minute?
    No.

This morning she swept up the sticky broken glass. Emptied
the ashtrays. Then heard stomp stomp stomp up the rickety
stairs. The Mounties. Enter my gracious home, gentlemen.
One of them tripped against the bottles. Nerve rattling glass
against glass. Sticky sounds on the floor from their thick shiny
shoes.
    When they left she started shaking. Splinters of memory
glinting in strong sunlight, glass shrapnel, searchlights. A
horse, a hand on a clothesline. Ice cubes swirling in crystal
glasses. Old movies where time passes with a whirlpool across
the screen. Grey swirls like muddy batter being stirred.
    My mother is dead. Killed in her car. My mother is dead.
Chant the words to get them inside. Life's a bitch and then
you die. Green crème de menthe and Remy Martin. Blossoms
on the plum trees. She was a bitch and then she died.

Outside the kitchen window, cars raced towards downtown.
Two solid lines headed east. Rushes of sound. Mechanical
tides controlled by stoplights. Distant sirens like gulls. The
garden full of brown and broken plants. The clothesline
empty, except for a couple of oily rags.

Her mother wears royal blue silk; there are pearls on her neck
and wrist.
   Mum, what are you doing?
   Can't you see? I'm hanging out the laundry.
   But it's all dry. You brought it in this morning.
   Her mother looks up, looks at the laundry. Feels the sheets.
Grasps the clothesline wire with her hands. Looks farther up,
cranes her neck at the clouds. Sighs.
   Does it really matter? Does it really matter what I do?

At home in Beresford the clothesline stretches across a small
ravine that leads down to the stream. The white laundry, like
tethered ghost costumes, used to flap between forest and
house. The sheets hung low enough that on the way down
to the stream, she could run right into them, fill her lungs
with their clean smell, then duck underneath and dash on.
So quiet down in the woods. Such small sounds. Sounds of
leaves being tapped with rain. Birds. The woodpecker. One
day a deer in the meadow. Like magic.

Hiding among the trees, I watch my mother hang out the
laundry. Me with my good eyes. Scout's eyes, Tonto eyes. She
stands above, on the wooden platform, feet in solid second
position, a pile of wet clothes in the wicker basket beside her. She
looks silly wearing a pink silk suit to do it. Drip, drip onto the
wooden platform.
   My mother's pale hands with their bright pink nails deliber-
ately separate the sopping garments and pin them with wooden

clothes pegs. She economizes, pins two pieces together with one peg, shoulder to shoulder, corner to corner. Joins them all together. Pin, wheel out; pin, wheel out. The line squeaks, and Peg watches the water drip down into the ravine from the white sheets and her father's white shirts.

Silence and bottles and echoes at home in Beresford. The piano standing idle, top locked and keyboard closed. No music coming in or going out. Just her mother's unsteady steps from room to room, all through the day and often the night.

You don't play much these days, Peggy.

I don't want to.

That wouldn't make your father very happy.

What do you know. What do you care. You didn't care about what made him happy.

Before heading for the airport, she walked across the street to her rock by the river. Turned back and looked over traffic up at the house, wondered if Monica saw her out the window, wondered if she heard or saw the Mounties come and go. She turned back and watched the water move steadily by. Winter coming. Snow. Ice. Grey. In another month or two, the river will darken, become laden with doilies of ice. The ice will start forming on the bottom, too, frog jelly layers gradually reaching up to the surface. Winter. Snow. The smoke from buildings will barely rise, will hover and hesitate at the roofs, hating to come out of the warm. Then the Bow River will

156

freeze over completely, and stones will bounce on its surface. The water will have to be imagined rushing along under the ice. Always strong, always moving.

Like Monica.

Except with the river you have a remote idea of what to expect when.

You didn't tell me a thing about it, Monica. You went behind my back.

Peg, I—

Forget it.

A die-hard fisherman stood in the middle of the river, rubber leggings up to his crotch. She could see his breath as he cast, cast again.

She and her father would escape in early mornings still foggy, Peg sleepy and curled up against him until they came to the border.

The big salmon burst from the sea and twisted in the air before the net came up under it. Shiny, clean fish. Fish knocked on the head with one good thunk and laid on ice. Hefted proudly up by the gills for a picture. Brought home and gutted in the carport; surgeon's hands slit the bellies and slid the red guts into a white bucket.

She leaned over the edge of the boat, felt each wave push against her middle. Her father's hat down over his eyes, a can of beer in his hand. They stayed that way for a long time. Then he sighed. He tipped his head back, looked up at the sky, and then down at the floor of the boat. Fingered the beer can. Dented it with his fingertips.

She wished it could be just the two of them forever and ever. They would live on a houseboat and catch fish. She would go ashore and dig clams, gather maple buds and fiddleheads. The fighting between her parents would cease, her mother would melt away, her mother who started in on him the moment he came in the door and kept at him, kept at him, who made him want to stay away long hours. If her mother disappeared, he would come home to just her.

The man caught a small whitefish, grey in the grey light. It twisted pitifully on the end of the line; it barely jumped out of the water. He unhooked it with his red hands and threw it back. And cast again. Right away he caught another, had trouble getting it off the line. Yanked. Tossed it into the air away from him in a gesture of revulsion. Wiped his hand on his leg.

She sees her father's car turn in the driveway, gallops home to him. Runs in with her riding boots still on. Runs in breathless even as he takes the two steps down into the living room, where her mother stands, slyly pleased, arms akimbo, fingers tapping flesh.

Well, Martin, what do you think?

His face flushes red and he shouts. His fingers clench the piano's curve. He lurches and buckles in pain and the lid of the

piano crashes down. All the strings sound together.
Martin?
Martin?

Her father's body lay in a pewter grey coffin at the front of the
church. Pitying eyes bored into her back. She could not avoid
looking at him. Painted like a mannequin. She moved her eyes
to the altar. In Remembrance of Me.
     Her mother elegant. Vogue *picture of bereavement in black*
lace and silk. A thin veil of ice on her skin and her words.
Afterwards the people came home, chatted and ate bakery cakes
and pastries, drank tea and coffee and sherry. In the dining room,
and in the living room beside the piano. Like a goddamn party,
she thought. There was even laughter. She saw her mother smile.
Saw her rest her arm on the piano. Hated her. Swore to her father
she'd never forgive.

She crossed the road from the river. Slid a note under
Monica's door. Called the cab. Started home.

Sixteen or seventeen: outside the tall windows is Beresford,
where's she's stuck for the time being. Inside, though, is
Broadway. Eartha Kitt's mauve face on the record album is
sexy. The picture is *bad,* and Peg loves it, loves Kitt's sensu-
ous, sultry voice. She makes up gestures to go with 'My Heart
Belongs to Daddy' and watches her reflection in the plate

glass. Leans forward and wiggles her ass. Da-dada, Da-dada-Daddy. She strokes her arms and wraps them round her and fingertips new curves from thigh to breast. She slides down to the floor and twists, climbs to her knees and holds her breasts together. Dad-dada-da-dada-daddy. She kisses the air with lips she hopes are pouty:

I simply adore
Your asking for more
But my heart belongs to Daddy.

Get up. What do you think you're doing?

Just fooling around.

You look cheap.

I *said*, I'm just fooling around.

You can get into trouble that way. You will take messages with your body out of this house and parade them on the street whether you know it or not.

Bitch bitch bitch bitch bitch. Get off my case. Mind your own business.

You've been stealing my liquor, haven't you?

No.

A whole bottle is missing. Now where do you suppose it is? Wherever could it be? You are far too young to be drinking, my girl.

Bitch.

What did you say?

I didn't touch your booze.

In the basement the boxes labelled 'Martin' in green felt pen are neatly stacked. She opens 'Shirts' and 'Sweaters' and takes the things she likes, the things she remembers he liked. Takes only jeans and underwear of her own. All packed in his leather bag.

She's a cat burglar breaking out. Runs in heavy unbalanced steps, his suitcase thumping against her side, through the heavy dew, down the dark green scallops of the driveway. On the silent wet road she listens for cars. This is it. This is it.

The bus leaves at midnight. The night is pitch. The mountains loom huge and sinister, blackening the black.

She has x.o. in her bag. Best bottle in the house. Bon Voyage. Au revoir. She ducks her head down, sneaks swallows. Lies over two seats and glowers when other people get on. Everyone leaves her alone, and she drinks that way.

In the morning when the mountains fall away, and the Appaloosa foothills recede and reappear in the distance, when the bus leaves the trees and heads onto the flat openness, she feels fear. Everything intensely unfamiliar, grey, as though the entire landscape is coated in dust. Longing for home hits her. Longing for the vine maples sprite green with new shoots in a tangle by the creek. Lacy ferns and big Boston ferns with spores bright coloured like bugs underneath each leaf on each frond. Skunk cabbages' flat green leaves, smelly golden temples housing bumpy yellow cocks.

Grey, it seems. Flat. Another planet.

But her mother will be glad to be left in peace with her gardens, her house, and her bottles. Sleeping on the chaise longue. Posturing by the roses. Free to wander around cursing or crying, wailing or sighing, bothering no one, and sure as hell no one bothering her.

Her legs are sore from sitting so long; she is sick of the smell of the bus; she is hungry. The Calgary bus depot is crammed with leaving and arriving, boxes and bags. She drinks styrofoam coffee in the cafeteria. Scans the classifieds. No idea how to start; not a clue. Calgary just the name of a place, she just a person in that place.

A plump girl in a pink and yellow sari plunks down across from her. She's holding a piece of lemon meringue pie. Do you mind? she asks, grinning. Her teeth are very white. She isn't Indian at all. She's fair. She has a diamond in her nose.

No. She lifts the paper.

I'm Monica. She is playing with a silver capsule on a chain around her neck, tipping it back and forth.

What's in there?

Mercury. I'm Gemini. She waves her fingers in front of her face. Talisman. Protection against evil. All of it. What are you looking for?

Somewhere to live.

Well well. I can help you there. Want a bite?

No.

I love it. I love this pie I do I do. I know. It *looks* like I love

it, right? Well so what. That's what I say. I happen to be fond
of flesh. Even my own.

Oh.

There are two apartments in the attic of the old yellow house.
Monica lives in one. Across the hall is Peg's. Both are small,
hindered by the slant of the roof. Peg steps in. Inside is a small
gas heater. A pot of water, coated with mineral residue, sits
on top. A bed, a couch, and a chair crouch under the strong
slope of the ceiling. No windows facing west.

The clawfoot tub in the bathroom has been painted bur-
gundy. Your very own bloodbath, says Monica. Maybe someone got murdered in here, and they put him in the bathtub,
and then when they snuck him out to bury him, they couldn't
get the stain out so they had to paint it. She laughs. Or maybe
someone committed suicide. I've heard about people slitting
their wrists in bathtubs.

Just shut up, would you? You're giving me the creeps.

Sorry. Drama major, you know. Now. What's next? Job,
right?

Physically, she is settled quickly. Monica lends her money
when she hasn't enough. Lends her a dress and drives her
down to the interview at the telephone company. Introduces
her to the cat who hangs out on their stairs.

After a month she writes to her mother. Everything is
fabulous; everything is fine. Hope you weren't too worried.

Her mother sends postcards in her wavering wobbling hand.

Good riddance.

Don't come to me for money.

How dare you take your father's things. Send them back. Send them all back.

I'm selling this place. I'm leaving.

Monica asks her over for drinks, weird cocktails she concocts. Joints. Occasionally Peg goes, plays a game of crib, or backgammon, but more often says no. Keeps to herself. Work and home. Work and home. Keep it simple at first. Keep alone. Don't need anyone. Prove you are not weak, but self-sufficient. Monica has helped too much already. Freedom is distance.

She dreams the woods at home are being demolished. Grey mud churns up over the rich black earth, up over the broken trunks and branches of trees. She hears chainsaws, gravel trucks. Her mother stands on the deck of a huge white steamer. She waves a long chiffon scarf.

Her father's death is played over and over again like a stuck record. Martin? click. Martin? click. Always always her mother's head thrown back in a diabolical laugh, cords in her throat tight; teeth big and white as an animal's; voice through a megaphone muffled and loud.

And she dreams about the man who is out to get her. Dreams he is creeping up on her, he is under the bed, he is at the window.

He appeared after she'd lived there two or three months. He doesn't go away. He lurks around the back steps, hides among the garbage cans. Either waiting for her to leave so he

can break in, or waiting for her to come home so he can rape
her and kill her. There is only one door, with a deadbolt, and
the windows are painted shut. But if she can imagine it, it
can happen.

One day she comes home from work and finds her underwear drawer empty. No panties. No bras. Gone. In panic, in
sweating fear, she knows he has taken it, is smelling the
crotches or dancing around wearing it, hairy belly and lace.
He'll be back for the rest of her. The phone rings and she
won't answer, watches it, trembling. She finds her things out
on the line. She'd forgotten.

Liquor helps her sleep, though it makes her fat. Drunk,
she doesn't care about anything. If he comes and kills her,
fine. If she gets big as a hippo, fine. Nobody is going to love
her anyway.

Drinking helps, she is sure. Makes her mind rest when it
whirls too much; forces her to slow down. Lifts her above the
earth and covers her with bright green leaves. Temporarily.
Then yanks her down. Down to Jesus Aslan help me. Help me
not be weak.

Sometimes she crawls into bed with someone, someone
who is too drunk to notice or care how she is. Guys she picks
up at the bars near work. Young men in cheap grey suits with
white pinstripes; in dirty construction clothes, in security
guard uniforms. Men who don't talk much, or if they do, say
nothing that matters.

The face above breathes liquor into hers. He thrashes
around on top of her, turns her this way and that. Sweaty

flesh slaps against her. Fucks her. He pants and moans and she lies wondering why it makes her so sad. Something is wrong. With her. She gets up and leaves in the middle of the night, stumbles her way home. Crawls, sometimes, to the apartment door, tries and tries to get the goddamn key into the goddamn lock, tries so hard to open the door, get inside. All those unnavigable stairs; all that darkness.

Mornings when she is hungover and ashamed the weight of her body seems to increase. She can lie with her eyes closed and feel her body bulge out, know her limbs are massive with thick flesh, each arm a leg, each leg an elephant's. Feel the stranger's sticky come between her legs. Hot, hated.

She starts to wake up crying. She is unable to be strong. She is failing.

One morning she simply breaks, and cannot stop crying. She lies on the couch and sobs. She cries all morning and afternoon. Stares at her distorted face in the mirror and is afraid for herself. What is the matter with you?

By five o'clock she is exhausted, and still she cries. Stares blankly at the tiny room, at the shawl that covers one dirty window. At the Bow's silent run beyond the window and the drive. She smokes one cigarette after another. At six she telephones her mother.

You have a penchant for melodrama, Peggy. You should have gone onto the stage.

Two bottles of red wine. The first works wonders; she is back in control. Is angry at herself for calling. There was no real need. She drinks most of the second bottle, but then knocks it over. The red wine makes a large dark splotch where it seeps into the dirty cracks in the wooden floor. She watches it and rocks herself. Starts crying again.

Soaked in wine and blood, she crawls across the hall and crumples outside Monica's door.

When they come back from the hospital, they sit on the chesterfield and Monica strokes her hair. Hush, lamb, hush. She holds her, rocks her back and forth.

Peg, Peg, you're so unhappy. You've got to let people know, dear one, so they can help. Why didn't you tell me? Why don't you talk to me?

Hey, hear my Streisand. People need people.

I'm so *lonely*.

Hush, lamb, I'll help. Just let me. She puts her hand on the bandaged wrist.

Next day Monica leaves a can of chicken soup outside her door. Then a pack of cigarettes. She starts soirées—they wear hats from her collection, hats covered with big flowers and tiny flowers, hats with feathers. Turbans with giant rhinestones, men's caps and fedoras, a bride's veil, a nun's headdress. They smoke pot, cigarillos, French cigarettes with gilt bands around ebony, blue, purple.

One day it is the Gatlin Brothers floating across the hall between their open doors, next it is Placido Domingo. Joplin, Crystal Gayle, Gilbert and Sullivan. Peg drinks far less. Loses some weight. Finds herself feeling genuinely *happy* every now and then.

Monica has theatre programs stapled to her walls. Prints

of nudes. Picasso's blue woman with her back turned behind the bathroom door.

I used to feel like that sometimes, Peg says. Like I wanted to curl into myself and away like that.

Protect your belly like a porcupine, smiles Monica. Perfectly natural, my dear. Just don't stay that way.

On their drives in the country, they sip caesars. Play classical music in the old Nash and wave celery sticks like batons. When they arrive at wherever, they turn off the music and whisper.

In the best photograph, Monica stands out on the prairie reaching up like a crazed evangelist. Thanksgiving, out near Balzac. Monica's aunt is sick, so they have cooked the dinner in their two ovens and taken it out to the men. Blue sky and yellow harvest. Horn of plenty. The flat yellow land stretching to the mountains.

They sit on the tailgate of an old green pickup, eat turkey and stuffing and mashed potatoes flooded with gravy from a Mason jar. The men's faces are black with dust; white eyes stare out. The men drink beer and crush the cans. They crunch the aluminum foil into balls and throw them at each other. Murmur their thanks and go back to work.

Monica and Peg stand on a bluff looking over a field of wheat. The grain ruffles in the wind, it's a pelt when an animal shivers.

Someday take me to see the sea, says Monica.

Okay. You have to. You have to see it.

Monica smiles. They are standing so close their breaths

meet. Monica looks at her with clear friendly eyes, puts her arms around her in a brief, warm embrace.

Tonight's hat is big and black velvet, graced with a perfect pink rose. She herself wears a red boa and red cloche. Your cocktail, madam, she says, and hands Peg a flute. Parfait Amour and Spanish champagne. Pour tu.

The room fills with jasmine incense and marijuana smoke. The light is blue, from a fringed shawl thrown over a pole lamp. They sit cross-legged on the floor and play backgammon.

Sex is supposed to be so great. But I almost hate it, you know? I think there's something wrong with me.

I doubt it. More like something wrong with the men.

Peg takes another toke. Stares, high, at the red and white backgammon discs and imagines hands stroking her, moving up her sides, running down her spine, arms pulling her toward him, not pushing her away.

What about you? I haven't seen you with any guys.

Monica looks at her and smiles. Right one hasn't come along, I guess. There are a lot of schmucks out there. Hey, you know, when I was living in Winnipeg and working as a masseuse, I had this priest who came to see me once a week. It was really good for him, I think. Here is this guy, not allowed to *really* touch and be touched. Only handshakes, pats on the shoulder. No real *touching.* Ever! Can you imagine? Coming to me was good for his soul. I'm sure of it. *You* should try it some time.

Back in her apartment, Peg thinks about the priest. Taking

those black and white clothes off his sacrosanct skin. How lonely.

A few days, a week or two later, she and Monica sit at the kitchen table, the curtains drawn, just one tall purple candle burning and glowing warm against the pink arborite. They share wine from the same pottery cup.

She is afraid to be seen naked. Her father's clothes, his woollen and chamois shirts, the heavy pullover sweaters hide her.

The game begins and piece by piece their clothing falls away. Unhook, unbutton, unclasp. Gently, gently. Cloth, pulled over heads, sliding off arms, falling down legs.

She sits across from her with her shirt off, while Peg is lifting hers up over her head. She drops it on the floor.

Hey, Monica says. Look at me.

The light brown skin on her shoulders and breasts glows in the candle's light.

She reaches across to her. Who put this table here? she says. Stands up and comes around behind her. Runs her hands up her arms, sweeps her hair back over her shoulders, up behind her head, moves her mouth to her neck. Thank God I got you out of those clothes, she whispers. It was like making passes at a man.

She clutches the base of the wine cup with one hand, clenches her upper arm with the other.

Let go, Monica says. Let go.

The touch along the curve of her hip bones, the reach

around her rib cage to her breasts. No idea it could be so loving like that, so gentle like that; no sense of what was inside her like that.

Home. That smell of home penetrates her shell. Tear-filled eyes as she heads out on the Deas Island thoroughfare. The smell of wet wool. She drives toward the border, through the tunnel, further, onto the clover leaf. Now over the grey concrete of Pacific Highway. Almost home, by the store, at the stop sign glass glitters on the road. The grass in the ditch is flattened. This is the place then. Where her mother died. The accident was here. Go on. Get going. Go on past the corner store, three hundred yards to go. There the driveway, lined with its scallops of lawn; rhododendrons and azaleas in strong green winter foliage parade up each side. The house not visible from the road. Turn up the driveway. Turn. No one's there.

The door squeaks open onto silence. Cool. Light and shadows mixed down the hallway. Hello? into nothing. I'm home. Words sucked into thick carpet. Down the chocolate hall. Past her bedroom. The room hasn't changed at all. Pale yellow flowers on the wallpaper, billowy white curtains on the windows. The clothes she left behind are still in the closet. Strange. Like seeing herself still hanging there.

Down the three steps into the living room, stepping into a museum or a church, stepping like a cat. Off-white carpets and raw silk furniture. The piano in the corner. Venetian blinds, drawn almost closed, tilted up so you can't see out.

It was the lightest room in the house when she left. Light poured through the tall plate glass windows, through the weave of the loose-woven curtains. The piano wears a shroud of beige lace. Royal Doulton ladies surround a rust chrysanthemum plant. A fern stands where her father died.

She likes to sit down at the piano right after he has played. The bench is still warm, the keys, even, are still warm. As though the wood, the keys, the strings, the very air around retains something of him. Even the sound she makes contains something of him.

Her mother painted the piano. With shiny cream-coloured paint to match the window sills. Painted over the dark rich luster of the wood with paint thick as half-whipped cream. Painted over 'Bosendorfer,' painted the three brass pedals.

Well, Martin? What do you think?

The decanters, newly filled, wait on the sideboard. She pours long fingers of Courvoisier into a snifter; sits on her mother's chaise-longue and inhales deeply before she sips. Breathe me in. I'll fix you. I'll help.

A picture of a woman in a garden hangs above the fireplace. She wears a long white dress, carries a small white parasol.

The young, flowering trees are white, the flowers at their base red. Daisies interrupt the green of the lawn.

The fireplace is empty and swept. Kindling is stacked in a neat pile on the grate, and there are four fat logs in front of the screen. Solid rows of leather-bound books rise on either side of the chimney. Emily Post. The Social Register.

She reaches and tips open the venetian blinds. The lawn is wet and green. She imagines her mother standing there, under the arbour in summer, tilting a rose's face up to hers. Carefully curved hands with colour-coordinated nails. That absent expression on her face. Cultivated peace. False tranquility.

Beyond the manicured grounds the woods are untouched, though the trees have grown; she can't see the stream from the house anymore. The firs and the row of cedars stand; the vine maples are leafless but the grey entwining trunks are there. All there, her forest, her wood. Soaked in rain, the brown fallen leaves shine. Feathery skeletons of dead ferns droop over the stronger green.

Where are you going?

I thought I'd come with you down to the creek, if that's all right.

Peg shrugs and goes ahead.

Her mother has on stupid shoes. She keeps getting branches caught in her hair, has to stop to disentangle herself, smooth her hair back into place.

Wait for me, Peggy.

Peg scoots ahead.

It is sort of pretty, in a wild sort of way. Maybe we could put a Japanese bridge across here. Would you like that?

No.

We could clear the brush away from the edge of the path to make it easier to walk.

No.

They stand staring at the stream for a few minutes. Twigs bob and bounce along its surface.

Well, don't say I didn't try.

—

I'd better be getting back.

Her mother steps off the wooden plank into the black mud. (For an instant it is quicksand; she lets her mother sink up to her neck; she begs to be pulled out.)

Her mother hired a gardener, a leathery thin man, a horrible man, with thick leather gloves. He cut prickly heaps of blackberry tendrils. He tore away the Oregon Grape and the huckleberry bushes from the driveway. Scalloped its edges. Planted lawn, azaleas, rhododendrons. Elizabeth, Carmen, Catalga; Lady Bligh, Madame Mason, Helen Close. Planted rose bushes at the grape arbour's feet. Eclipse, Fragrant Cloud, King's Ransom. Her mother stood on the clothesline platform and gestured dismissively at the woods. Later.

The black walnut tree stood in the centre of the lawn. Branches with eye-shaped green leaves on pliable wands joined by knuckles to the bigger branches. She picked these fronds and tucked them in her trousers, played wood nymph, sprite. She was sure she could fly from this tree, sure it required only want and will. And so she climbed, praying to Jesus and to Aslan as she climbed, as she shinnied out, as she closed her eyes and leapt.

That black walnut tree should come down, said the gardener. It blocks the sun. And anyways you don't want the little girl falling out again.

She hears voices on the lawn outside her window. Out her window she sees them. He has an orange chainsaw in his hand. Her mother stands beside him turquoise and pink, nodding, ringed hands on hips. Peg screams down the hall and out the door. Her mother grips her with iron claws. She rips herself away and runs. Down at the creek she hears the saw start up, hears it whine through tree flesh. Hears the crash.

In the night she prowls. Arms akimbo, she swirls the ice in her glass. Cat walk, Tonto walk in bare feet. Past the cellar door and a quick look down the stairs. She felt her way down those stairs the night she ran away from home. Felt with her hands the wood of the rail, the rough coldness of the uneven concrete walls. If you fell down here, you'd open your head against concrete. Bash. You'd lie crumpled at the bottom with broken glass all around, sticky shards still clutched in your bloody hand. Alone. Flies would crawl over glass and skin, sucking, licking, biting off sweetness from liquor and blood.

What's down there? Nothing she wants now. Cobwebs and dirt and dust. Mouse shit. Damp earth smell. Cold concrete floor and unfinished walls. The boxes of clothes in the farthest corner.

You take off his clothes. Her mother was pale; she was shaking. What are you doing in his clothes? Her voice rose and rose to a wail. She grabbed at the shirt, crying, her nails tearing flesh with the fabric.

No. Nothing.

Up and down through the living room the ghostly woman in white.

Outside, heavy rain rustles the leaves. Water rushes from a break in the eaves, splashes onto the wooden deck. She holds her glass up to the window, peers out into the dark ravine. Faint light is cast from the patio light, glistens on nearby trees.

She sits naked watching her belly and rocks back and forth on the edge of the bed. Watches the swirling patterns the melting ice makes in the scotch.

Shall I make the bed over top of you?

Yes! And she lies straight and still on her back with her eyes closed. Her mother shakes the clean white sheet out over her. It floats down and touches her face, brings with it a faint scent of outside, of cedars and pines. Then blankets, then the gold satin eiderdown. Her mother folds back the sheet.

What a pretty face hiding under here!

I'm dead. I can't hear you.

Are you? That makes me very sad. No more kisses from my precious daughter. No more tickling, like this.

Hahahaha! Mummy stop it!

More ice, more scotch to melt it. A small, happy cycle. Have faith in that. Have faith in that as you rock back and forth all alone.

She wakes shivering and thirsty. She's upside down, her feet on the wet pillow. The ashtray is full of soggy butts. The bedside table is covered with water from the ice cube tray. Didn't need ice at the end. Medicinal, those last gulps. Therapeutic. Her head is pounding. She hates herself. Backwards. I'm going backwards.

Hey hey! Let's move to the coast! I've been accepted at U.B.C. for grad school—see?
  You didn't tell me you were applying there.
  I didn't want to make waves in case I didn't get in.
  But now you do.
  Now I have to. Oh come on. It'll be great.
  No.
  Peg you've got to deal with your mother some time.
  Whoa. Shut up. And thanks a lot, by the way.
  Peg—
  Leave me alone.

Monica. There. Here. The world here is ghosts. Ghosts razor-edged in black like funereal calling cards. White paper bitten around the edges by sharp fire teeth. There is Monica, all Monica. Tangible and warm. Present or absent. Oh if she were here right now to hold her, she would move up against her warm back. She would run fingers up her moist spine. Kiss cubbyholes of collarbone. If she were here, she would know where to put her hands, her mouth.

Peg—

No.

Pound, water, pound. Wash away all trace of sin. The water gushes down onto her head, runs down her face, her breasts, her back. The water, her head, her heart beat loudly.

(Monica as unself-conscious as a man about her body. Utterly at ease in her flesh. Lying in the bathtub making her breasts and belly appear and disappear, water rising and falling and slapping against her skin like tides, up and down. Water trickling from her mossy pubic hair.)

Your mother couldn't have been all bad, Peg. Your Dad must have been doing something for her to be drinking like that.

You know nothing about it, Monica.

Peg makes herself a talcum powder ghost. Swipes the steam in a wide arc until she can see her white face in the mirror. Pale, unhappy ghost. Yanks on her jeans, her t-shirt, her father's shirt.

The air is cold this morning; the fog in the ravine is just lifting. She'd forgotten about the dampness on the coast, the dampness that wrinkles your clothes, that works its chilling way deep into you. She stands rocking on the sill of the French doors.

Hush, lamb. I love you.

Complete. True.

Don't blow it.

Crumpled at the bottom with broken glass all around, sticky shards still clutched in your bloody hand. Alone.

Raindrops tremble and threaten to fall from the clothesline wire. As she descends she kicks up the sodden leaves, smells cedar and rain. The vine maples have built hurdles, the path has faded, but she knows where it is; her body remembers.

Hemlock and new cedars have grown out of the mother stump; young cedar branches sweep gracefully down over the edge of the giant felled parent and almost touch the ground. No one ever came here but her. She could hear her mother call, but the muffled words were from so far away they were of another world. It was kind of like being drunk.

She peels the bark off a branch. Watches her breath hit the chill air.

She tears down the ravine. Heart racing she climbs the stump. Can't wait to drink. Loves the taste of scotch mints, or cherries, or chocolate. Loves the warmth coursing through her body. Sits on her stump and sings every song she knows. Becomes terribly, terribly brave.

I—You—

What's all that green around your mouth? Peggy?

She sways in the doorway. Hangs onto the door frame. Swings forward into the room.

Biiitch.

Go into their room. The heart of the house. Go in onto
soft smoothed carpet, way inside to mahogany and linen.
She ran here quiet and crying, bears and witches still
growling and grasping, their rough tickles churning her
stomach. Mummy. And in those days her mother loved
her, and she crawled into the warmth of the sheets and her
mother's soft stomach, and her mother stroked her hair as
she fell back to sleep.

On the dressing table is a picture. Her mother in her
twenties. Peg's dark hair. Peg's eyes. One other picture, of
her grandparents. Her grandmother a large grey and pink
shape with netting over her face. Her grandfather with his
icicle eyes and thin bony nose.

They didn't hug their daughter hello when they came to
visit, they just touched her on the shoulder, touched her
cheek with their lips. Patted Peg's head with brittle hands.
Shook distant hands with her father.

*Peg pushes open the door of the study. Her mother is tilted in
a funny way at the filing cabinet.*

What are you doing?

*Her mother jolts upright, lips and chin wet, invisible hands
screwing on a lid. She is crying. She slams the drawer shut.
Nothing. Coping. No.*

The sterling dressing set gleams on the boudoir table. The
center drawer is crammed with silk scarves; presents from her
father.

He wasn't a damned saint, for heaven's sake. He wasn't perfect.
He did things wrong.
  Like what?
  Never mind. Never mind.
  You're full of shit. And he never loved you.

Bedside drawers are filled with liquor miniatures, empty
and full. She takes them all out, rolls and clinks them
together on the bed. She lies down among them and they
roll against her.

Royal blue silk sweeps around her mother's calves; pearls at ear
and throat. Her father stands to one side, stands with his drink
as though he is still mingling at the party.
  You're not going to start this again, are you?
  How could you put me through that?
  I'm going to bed. I suggest you do the same. If you can make
it that far.
  And now women, too, Martin. How many women?
  Lana—
  I don't know how much more I can stand.
  Lay off the booze.
  It's you. You're a stone.
  You know where the door is.

Postured by her roses. Touched them as she named them.
White Queen, Peace, Blaze. Climbing roses. Crawling roses.
Lonely, lonely woman.

He never loved you.

I'm sorry.
   I'm so very sorry. Now. When you can't hear. When you're gone and I can't touch you, can't meet your eyes.

Her mother's clothes fill the closet from end to end. Bright colours, a penchant for silk; Singapore, Thai, watered, raw. Peg leafs through the clothes, pulls out a caftan that shimmers from red to blue like a fish. She stands for a minute regarding her naked self then slides the silk over her head. It slips cool down her body. She sweeps up her hair with silver brushes and fastens it with combs. Closes the door of the bedroom and watches this woman in the mirror, swishing this way and that, this human being naked underneath the glistening silk; watches that woman in the picture, that woman under glass.

Light streams in when she opens the blinds. She leans back on the chaise longue. Outside, a grey cat stalks along the edge of the lawn.

Monica, can you come? Could you come here?
   Yes.
   God how I miss you.

Below the clothesline, at the bottom of the ravine, the creek is full to the brim. It will overflow, eventually, and make swamps in the black earth. The water will not recede until spring, when it will leave moist plots for the skunk cabbages. Yellow violets will come, scattered below the vine maples with their wrinkly young leaves, and the firs will have tips of new green. Beneath the clothesline the dark mass of vines will be covered with purple stars. Lilies of the valley, trilliums in the woods. Then daffodils, and forget-me-nots. Her mother's gardens will explode into vibrant reds and pinks and yellows, planned and planted to reach from spring well through fall.

J. JILL ROBINSON is from Langley, B.C. Her stories have appeared in publications including *Event, NeWest Review, Secrets from the Orange Couch,* and *Prism international.* "Finding Linette" was a co-winner of *Event*'s Creative Non-Fiction Prize in 1992. Her first book, *Saltwater Trees,* was published by Arsenal Pulp Press in 1991. She has a B.A. and M.A. in English from the University of Calgary and an M.F.A. from the University of Alaska at Fairbanks. In 1987, she participated in the writing program at the Banff Centre for the Arts. She lives with her husband and two dogs in Calgary, where she is currently teaching part-time in the English Department at the University of Calgary.

SELECTED TITLES FROM
ARSENAL PULP PRESS

FICTION / POETRY
Company Town (Michael Turner) *$10.95*
Dog Years (Dennis Denisoff) *$11.95*
Higgledy Piggledy (Robin Skelton) *$13.95*
Saltwater Trees (J. Jill Robinson) *$11.95*
Shades (The Whole Story of Doctor Tin) (Tom Walmsley)
    $13.95
Songs of Aging Children (Ken Klonsky) *$11.95*

NON-FICTION
Canada Remapped (Scott Reid) *$14.95*
Guy's Guide to the Flipside (Guy Bennett) *$10.95*
*The Imaginary Indian: The Image of the Indian in
    Canadian Culture* (Daniel Francis) *$15.95*
The Little Black and White Book of Film Noir (Peg
    Thompson and Saeko Usukawa) *$4.95*
A Little Rebellion (Bridget Moran) *$12.95*
*Whispered Art History: Twenty Years at the Western
    Front* (Keith Wallace) *$24.95*

Available from your local bookstore, or prepaid directly
(please add $1.00 per book for shipping + 7% GST in
Canada) from the address below:

ARSENAL PULP PRESS
100-1062 Homer Street
Vancouver, B.C. Canada V6B 2W9

Write for our free catalogue.